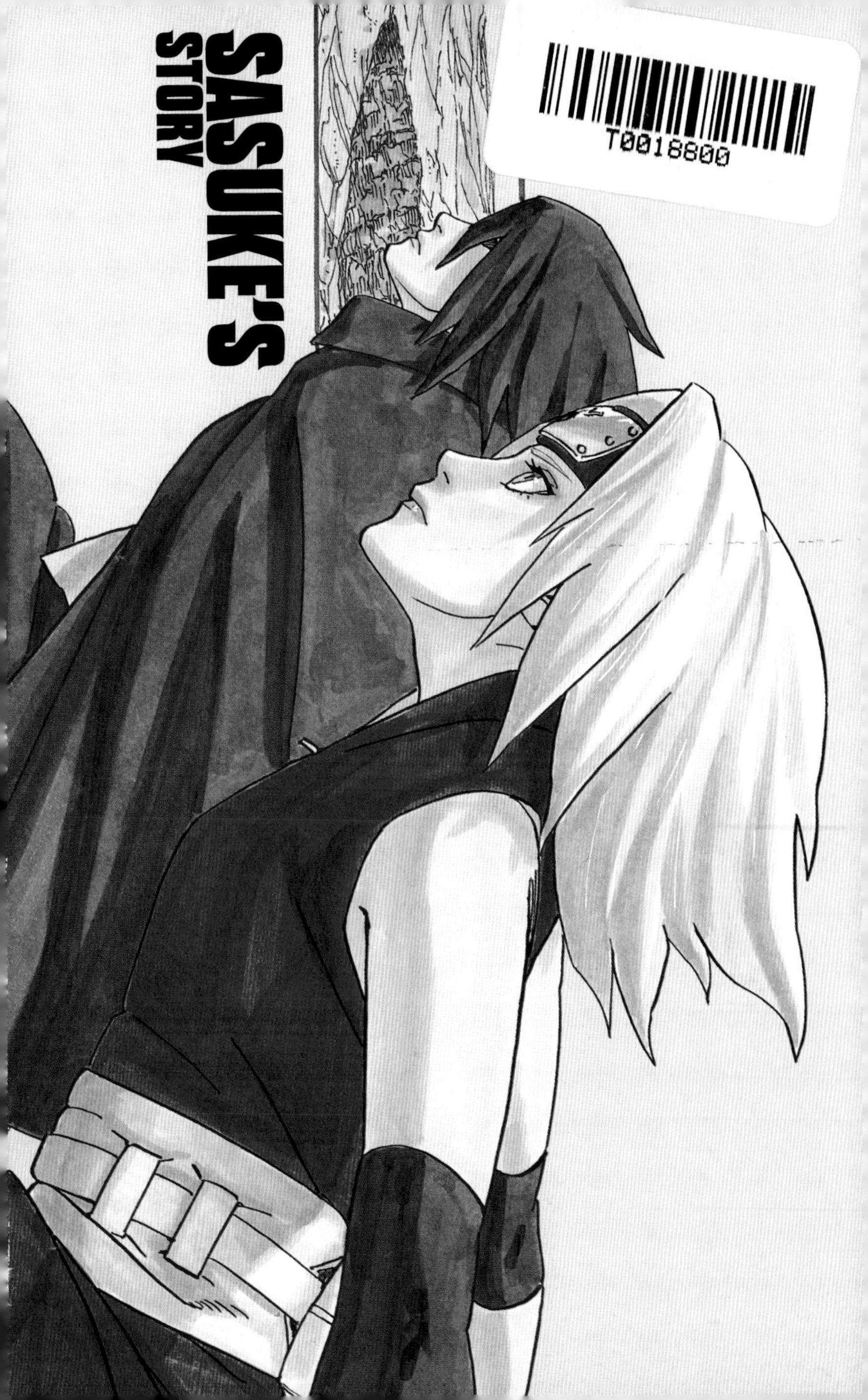
SASUKE'S
STORY
T0018800

NARUTO

SASUKE'S STORY

The Uchiha
and the Heavenly Stardust

Masashi Kishimoto
Jun Esaka

CHARACTERS

Uchiha Sasuke

Master of the kekkei genkai Sharingan. Former member of Team Seven. Sakura's husband.

Uchiha Sakura

User of medical ninjutsu. Former member of Team Seven. Sasuke's wife.

Zansul

Director of the Astronomical Research Institute. He was given a critical mission by the Land of Redaku prime minister.

Meno

A jailer in the form of an enormous lizard who guards the Astronomical Research Institute.

Jiji

A prisoner sharing a cell with Sasuke and doing hard labor at the Astronomical Research Institute.

CONTENTS

COVER + INTERIOR DESIGN Shawn Carrico
TRANSLATION Jocelyne Allen

Published by VIZ Media, LLC
P.O. Box 77010
San Francisco, CA 94107

Library of Congress Cataloging-in-Publication Data

Names: Esaka, Jun, author. | Kishimoto, Masashi, 1974- creator. | Allen,
Jocelyne, 1974- translator.
Title: Sasuke's story. The Uchiha descendants and the heavenly stardust /
Jun Esaka, Masashi Kishimoto ; translation, Jocelyne Allen.
Other titles: Sasuke retsuden. Uchiha no matsuei to tenkyū no hoshikuzu.
English | At head of title: Naruto
Description: San Francisco, CA : Viz Media, 2022. | Series: Naruto |
Summary: "Uchiha Sasuke heads for an astronomical observatory far from
the Land of Fire where he joins up with Sakura and dives into an
undercover investigation to search for traces of the Sage of Six Paths!
There, they discover a plan that goes beyond life and death."-- Provided
by publisher.
Identifiers: LCCN 2022018530 (print) | LCCN 2022018531 (ebook) | ISBN
9781974732586 (paperback) | ISBN 9781974735686 (ebook)
Subjects: CYAC: Fantasy. | Ninja--Fiction. | LCGFT: Light novels.
Classification: LCC PZ7.1.E816 Sap 2022 (print) | LCC PZ7.1.E816 (ebook)
| DDC [Fic]--dc23
LC record available at https://lccn.loc.gov/2022018530
LC ebook record available at https://lccn.loc.gov/2022018531

Printed in the U.S.A.
First printing, November 2022

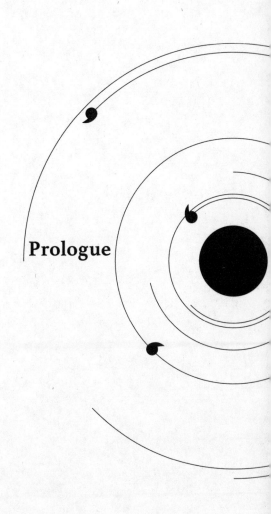

Prologue

The man couldn't sleep.

He sank his skinny body deeper into the cold sheets. He was indoors, but he could see his breath puff white clouds, and he couldn't stop shivering, no matter how tightly he wrapped himself in the threadbare blanket.

He'd been sleeping on this thin, sweat- and grime-stained futon for almost two weeks. Each day he woke with more bruises than the day before, which made him feel he'd hardly slept at all. Maybe he could have gotten some rest in a room where the wind didn't blow and whistle through the cracks in the walls.

The man bitterly lifted his heavy eyelids and peered into the dark room.

There were four grown men sleeping on the floor alongside each other. The room was small, with space for maybe six tatami mats, about nine square meters. Seniority counted for a lot here, so as the newcomer, he'd been given the coldest spot to sleep in. He couldn't protest.

"Dammit," he groaned as he rolled over on the hard floor. "How did I end up here?"

Two weeks earlier, he was imprisoned in the capital city of the Land of Redaku. But even as a prisoner, he'd been granted the bare minimum of a life there. That prison was so comfortable he'd even considered committing another crime when his sentence was up just to get himself sent back.

However, one day out of the blue, he got transferred. He was told only that he would be doing construction work in the north. With the work being physical labor, only young and healthy prisoners were being sent.

In the end, he had been brought to a facility made of stone on the peak of a desolate mountain.

The Tatar Observatory.

The historic facility took its name from the legendary astronomer Jean-Marc Tatar, who had lived at the same time as the Sage of Six Paths—supposedly. He was disinterested in any of that lore though. His concern was the location of the facility that he was in, a region so cold that temperatures remained below freezing even as spring approached. The prisoners were kept in an environment and condition worse than what stock animals had to endure, in terms of food, room, and clothing. And they were forced to hack away at the cold earth from morning until night with hardly a break of any kind.

"Why...do I have to..."

He gritted his chattering teeth and clutched the edge of his blanket. His dirty nails dug into the palms of his hands, and his skin had peeled away from the successive days of intense physical labor.

His crime had been robbery and murder. One winter's day three years earlier, when he hadn't known where his next meal would come from, he forced his way into a house and stole everything he could sell. When he fled, he left the young couple who owned the house and their two children tied up inside. But no one had come along to free them, and the family froze to death two days later.

Four people dead because of him. He could hardly bear the thought. He had stolen from them only because he didn't have anything to eat, so in his mind his theft was an act of self-defense. He hadn't meant to kill anyone.

Why did this have to happen to me?

Dissatisfaction filled his heart, slowly but surely. He had had enough. Staring at the grain of the wooden ceiling planks, the man made his decision.

Once day breaks, I'm getting out of here.

The prisoners' lives were controlled by a gong.

When the dull *gong gong* sounded at the crack of dawn, the exhausted prisoners would rise like zombies. If they overslept, the patrolling guards never hesitated to use their truncheons mercilessly, so the prisoners were always very quick to climb out of their futons. They filed out of their cells, wiping away the sleep in their eyes and scratching incessantly at arms covered in rashes.

Meals were twice a day. Vegetables and barley boiled to within an inch of their lives—slop not even a pig would eat.

Joining the line that snaked out of the dining hall, the man took a deep breath and tried to calm himself and the intense feelings that flooded him.

His body was heavy with exhaustion, but his mind was sharp and excited. He could not be bothered by anything that morning, not the man who cut ahead of him in line and stepped on his foot, nor the man behind him clearing his throat of something so loud it felt like it would land in his ear.

Today he would leave this place. He was breaking out.

The man picked up his breakfast tray and looked out at the room crowded with prisoners. For his escape, there was someone he wanted to invite along.

The shoddy room—a cafeteria in name only—was lined with rickety tables and chairs that were nothing more than chopped logs.

The person he was looking for was sitting in his usual seat near the window.

Prisoner No. 487. Sasuke.

More unusual than his name was his appearance. Unadulterated black hair and eyes. The chiseled fine lines of his face, a proud nose and a profile that drew the eye. His features composed a perfect picture not just from the front but from any angle whatsoever. When he saw him up close, the man wondered if they were really the same species.

Though born with such looks, Sasuke was silent and unfriendly, always aloof like a cat, which only drew more attention to him.

Even more annoying was his strength—so strong was he that no one could lay a hand on him.

On Sasuke's first day at the facility, the old hands had been quick to harass the unusual newcomer. But seconds later, they were crawling along the ground with dislocated joints. As the men cried out in extreme pain, Sasuke had looked down on them. The warning that came from his mouth was quite simple: "Leave me alone."

The majority of prisoners found Sasuke difficult to approach. The man himself should have felt the same way, but on that day when he'd made up his mind to escape, he found the ability to speak to the intimidating stranger.

He sat down across from Sasuke and opened his mouth.

"Er. Um." The voice that had sounded clear and strong in his mind came out weak and timid. "So, um. You're...a-a shinobi too, right?"

Sasuke shifted his gaze from the window to the man. "What do you want?"

Caught by those black eyes, his core trembled. "I-I. Uh. I mean, I am too. From the Land of Wind. I didn't manage to graduate from the academy though, and my parents gave up on me. So I ended up drifting to this country. I can still knead chakra though. See?"

Using his chakra, he drew the tip of a chopstick to him and made it wobble.

He looked at Sasuke boldly, with a meaningfully arched eyebrow, but the black eyes had already lost interest and turned back to the window.

So you're ignoring me?

He stifled the urge to click his tongue and glared at Sasuke. He couldn't have been any great shinobi seeing that he'd been taken prisoner in a remote country like this.

As Sasuke stared out the window, he moved his chopsticks neatly from the bamboo shoots to the dish of fiddleheads on the flattened steel tray before him. He was an unfriendly man, but his manners revealed his good upbringing. He was quite obviously different from the human garbage that made up the prison population; anyone could see it.

"W-would you join up with me?" the man said, after waiting for Sasuke to finish eating. He was nervous and stammered the question.

"What do you mean?" Sasuke asked coolly.

"Escape," the man replied. "W-we get out of here. You can control ch-chakra, right? Um, th-the two of us...could climb the wall and escape."

The observatory was surrounded by a wall of stone about ten meters high. Looking up at it from the ground, it seemed impossibly huge, but it wasn't so tall as to be unclimbable, not if they used chakra.

"I-I've had enough of this place," the man continued. "Y-you must be fed up too, right?"

Sasuke looked at him, no expression on his face. "What do you know about me?"

"I know that you're no ordinary man." Finally, he was able to say his piece without stammering.

He couldn't figure out what a man like Sasuke could have done to end up in a place like this. Even so, he could hardly believe that the cool stranger was satisfied with these endless days of boring labor.

"You and me, we escape," he said again. "Everyone's heading out to their morning jobs now, right? So we jump over the wall in the chaos of people coming and going."

"Give it up," Sasuke told him curtly. "There's nothing but wasteland on the other side of that wall. It would take two days to walk to the nearest town. You'd just collapse on the road."

"W-we could pick wild vegetables, fruit, as much as we wanted. We could eat a million times b-better than the slop in here," the man persisted. "And look, it's all foggy out. If we're going to give Meno the slip, it's gotta be to—"

"I warned you," Sasuke said, glanced out the window, and then stood up with his empty tray.

The prisoners standing and chatting in the narrow aisle hurriedly stepped aside to make a path when they saw Sasuke coming.

The man chased after him and grabbed Sasuke's arm. "Don't you want to get out of here?!"

Sasuke easily shook his hand off. "Sorry. I'm here because I want to be."

The man was dumbfounded. "What?"

Here because he wants to be?

The man gaped as Sasuke left the cafeteria.

He waited until the cool stranger was out of sight and then kicked at the table.

Making me look like a fool. Well, fine. You can rot in this hellhole. I'm going to be free.

The man scarfed down the rest of his breakfast and stormed out into the hallway. He marched outside past prisoners talking with each other and looked up at the wall.

There was still time before the day's work started. The likelihood of any sentries posted outside at this moment was infinitesimal.

No one kept an eye on the wall. Unlike in prison, the guards here only watched over the prisoners at work. They scoffed at the idea that anyone could climb the ten-meter wall with zero footholds.

Too bad for them. I can climb it.

The man gently placed his palms on the smooth stone. Remembering the lessons he'd had in the past, he kneaded his chakra and concentrated it in his palms.

He felt his skin suction to the surface of the stone, and the man began to crawl straight up the vertical wall like a frog.

He could hear the prisoners making noise off in the distance. It had been only a couple minutes since he started to climb. There weren't too many people outside at this time of day. The director and the sentries were no doubt eating their breakfast in the main building.

You're fine. You can do this. You can climb it before they notice you. As long as Meno doesn't show up.

His body was much lighter than he'd imagined. He was already halfway to the top, but he wasn't tired at all. He felt like he could keep climbing for another hour.

Krnch.

The man heard footsteps on the gravel below, and he looked down at the ground. His eyes fixed on a pair of yellow eyes, and suddenly all the hair on the back of his neck stood on end.

"...!"

Meno had found him.

Bad, bad, bad. I have to hurry!

Panicking, the man lost control of his chakra. His suctioned hands slipped, and his body fell backwards into the air.

He barely realized he was falling when he felt a fiery pain erupt in his side.

His blood pressure plummeted. As his mind faded to darkness, he met Meno's eyes once more and saw fangs sunk deep into his stomach.

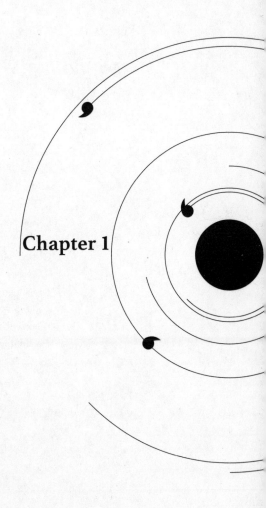

Chapter 1

Teeth still plunged into the man's body, Meno dropped to the ground lightly. He opened his mouth, and the body fell out.

"Unh..."

The man tried to crawl away, but Meno stepped on him and violently flipped him over. He caught the man's shoulder blade with the sharp claws of his forelimbs and dragged him out to the courtyard. Here he stopped, opened his bright red mouth, and bit into the man's shoulder.

"Aaaaah!" the man shrieked and threw his head back.

His flesh ripped open, and the blood gushed and mixed with the blood still pouring from his stomach, creating a bloody pool on the ground.

Meno could have ripped the man's head off or dug into his chest, giving him a swift death, but he instead turned the man once more and raked his claws down his back, pulling out threads of muscle.

Face pressed into the dirt, the man wept wretchedly.

Meno took his time with the would-be escapee and deliberately dragged the man into the courtyard so that he and this moment would be in full view of the other prisoners. It was a show, a message to the rest of the prisoners that they would meet the same fate if they also tried to escape.

"Whoa, harsh."

"He's still alive. Poor guy."

The prisoners frowned as they watched from a distance while they shouldered their pickaxes.

Appearing to delight in shredding the man's flesh, Meno at last began disembowelment. As the prisoners heard the slow dripping of wet guts and organs, the man's miserable cries finally fell silent.

"Okay, that's enough rubbernecking. Get to your posts already."

The workers flinched in sync when they heard this low voice from behind.

A slender man in silver-rimmed glasses strolled out of a building. Zansul, director of the Tatar Observatory and the person ultimately in charge there, and Meno's master.

"If you don't hurry and get to work, I'll give you to Meno for his dessert." Zansul's tone was casual but carried a note of intimidation that sent shivers down spines.

The prisoners grew very pale. They quickly scattered to take up their posts, and mixed among them, Sasuke secretly took a long look at Meno.

Leaning forward to bury his face in the skinned stomach before him, Meno waved his long tail back and forth for balance. The hard skin that covered his face was painted red, and his yellow eyes flashed brightly.

A carnivorous jailer loyal only to director Zansul—that was Meno. The giant bipedal lizard had thick skin covered in keratin, teeth like steel wedges, and razor-sharp claws. He was about two and a half feet when standing and walking, but, measured from the top of his head to the tip of his tail, he was more than six and a half feet long. His legs grew straight down from his torso and were like powerful springs, allowing him to travel almost a hundred feet in a single leap.

The observatory was different from a prison. The sentries didn't keep watch over the prisoners every second of the day like jailers, and there were no locks on the cells or the front door of the building where the prisoners lived. There was no need for locks, and the reason was Meno.

Meno was a threatening guardian who watched over the premises and mercilessly killed and ate any prisoner who broke the rules, and so the prisoners were very obedient. And almost no one came forward with thoughts of escaping.

The work of the prisoners was mainly to dig. With hoes used for farm work, they hacked away at the frosted earth. When they came across a large stone or hard chunk of earth, they carefully dug it up and removed it from the ground. Rinse and repeat.

Apparently, the digging was necessary to construct a foundation for a massive telescope, but the long-time prisoners said that they had been digging for nearly a year now with nothing in particular to show for it.

"Aah, I'm freezing." Jiji stood his hoe up against his side and rubbed his hands together briskly.

The cold was especially biting in the mornings, to the point where any snot running from noses would freeze up before having a chance to fall.

"Sasuke, you're not cold?" he asked of the man working next to him.

"I am," Sasuke replied honestly and rubbed the handle of his hoe with the palm of his hand, relishing the meager warmth generated by the friction. He was used to missions in cruel environments, but cold was cold.

"Aah, it's too much. Why do they need an observatory in a place so freezing cold? The snow's long melted back in Nagare.

I'm telling you, we keep this up and we'll freeze to death sooner or later. But if the alternative's getting ripped apart and eaten like that fellow this morning, it might actually be better to freeze to death in my sleep."

Nose red, Jiji rambled on and on, no doubt tired of the monotonous work.

He was also a prisoner at the institute and shared a cell with Sasuke. He'd been arrested for stealing when he didn't have anything to eat and given a minimum sentence of six months. He was around the same age and build as Sasuke, so they had been assigned to the same work area and often ended up paired together.

"Ah!" Jiji suddenly cried out, as he rubbed the tips of his fingers together. "Crap, I busted a blister. Oh, but wait. That's actually lucky! Now I can go to the infirmary."

"What's at the infirmary?" Sasuke asked.

"You don't know? New lady doctor. I hear she's a real beauty and real nice to boot." Grinning, Jiji added, "Single too. No significant other."

Sasuke cocked his head to one side. "How do you know she's single?"

"Well, she's not wearing a ring, so."

A ring?

Sasuke stared uncomprehendingly.

"Oh, right!" Jiji said. "You're from another country. I forgot. It's the custom in the Land of Redaku, okay? When you get married, you exchange rings. A ring on the fourth finger of the left hand, that means you're married. And this lady doctor, she's got no ring—Oh, crap. Guards."

Jiji cut himself off when he noticed the approaching sentries, repositioned his hands on his battered hoe, and pulled it along the ground, pretending to work diligently.

The guards twirled their truncheons ostentatiously and glared at Jiji but didn't even meet Sasuke's eyes. They were afraid of him.

As the patrol moved on, Jiji released his hoe, and the breath he'd been holding came out in a white cloud. "Aah, I'm tired. I'm cold. I just can't anymore."

Sasuke agreed. He looked back with a sigh.

The Tatar Observatory stood on the peak of a range of rocky mountains. Built at an altitude of 16,400 feet, it was a tightly guarded stone jail. And *the* Sage of Six Paths was said to have stayed there.

To find a record of the Sage's stay at the observatory—that was Sasuke's objective.

In the Land of Fire, Naruto was suffering from an illness. And the only thing Sasuke could do to help him was to scrape together any records the Sage of Six Paths left in this land.

He was frustrated that this was the one time when he couldn't do anything else for his friend. Naruto grew sicker every second Sasuke spent here...

"What's wrong?" Jiji called out to him. "That's some look on your face." Beneath a mane of hair left to grow freely, the almond eyes of his cellmate were inscrutable to him.

Sasuke was yanked out of his own thoughts. "Oh, it's nothing."

"You sure? You looked real serious there."

"I'm fine." Sasuke brushed him off and readjusted his grip on the hoe.

Returning to his cell after supper, Sasuke had set a hand on the iron bars of his cell door and was welcomed with a discouraged cry.

"Aaaah!"

A small skinny man lay prostrate on the floor in the middle of the room. Penzila, one of Sasuke's three cellmates. Jiji sat cross-legged in front of him, and a teacup and some dice lay between the two men.

"Damn you, Jiji!" Penzila cried. "Rolling doubles!"

"Sorry. I'll be taking those cigarettes, thank you." Jiji grinned and pulled the cigarettes on the floor toward him.

They were playing Cee-lo.

Given that their confined lives lacked any entertainment, many prisoners were obsessed with games of chance. But Penzila had been addicted to gambling in the outside world as well. And while he might have been fanatical about it, he wasn't actually very good at it, which led him to acquire some serious debts after a series of losses. He had gone on to commit one marriage fraud after another, targeting women of wealth and using their money to repay those debts until he was finally arrested. A minimum of one year in prison.

"Oh, Sasuke! Come play Cee-lo with us!" Penzila rattled the dice in the teacup when he noticed Sasuke. He had clearly still not learned his lesson.

Sasuke shook his head. "I'm good."

"Come on. You're no fun," Penzila groaned and twisted his head around to a corner of the room. "Ganno! You're playing, yeah? Quit with the drawing and get over here already."

In a corner of the room, Sasuke's third cellmate, Ganno, crouched over like a bird with an egg, his back turned to Penzila. "I can't now," he replied curtly.

In his mid-sixties, Ganno was by far the oldest person in the prison. There was a bit of red paint smudged on the hanging skin at the nape of his neck.

"You still doing that?" Penzila asked. "You never get sick of it?"

"Don't talk to me," Ganno told him. "I'm at an important bit, almost finished."

A month ago, when Ganno went out to work, he'd returned suddenly with his pockets full of reddish-brown stones. "I found something good," he told his cellmates. He had then spent every free moment slamming those rocks together to smash them to pieces, regardless of how the work cut into the skin of his hands. When he had finally broken all the stones after a full five days, he started to peel away the skin on the soles of his feet. Then he had asked the group in charge of meals for a pot and a spot at the hearth. And over nearly two weeks, totaling thirty hours during his allotted breakfast hours, he boiled that peeled skin.

More than one person questioned his sanity as they watched Ganno wrap cloth around the bloody soles of his feet, but he seemed to be enjoying himself.

Ganno finally completed the thick broth made of his boiled skin and finished making the reddish-brown powder from smashing the rocks on the day Sasuke arrived at the observatory. Ganno had given a hurried hello to the newcomer, and then began to mix his two ingredients together on a matsubusa vine leaf. Sasuke watched his cellmate's hands as the man immersed himself in work Sasuke didn't really understand. Then he gasped.

When the thick liquid was mixed with the dark reddish-brown powder, it immediately became thicker and more viscous, taking on a glossy, rich mahogany color. Ganno continued to work the mixture for a few more minutes, and soon he had a vivid carmine pigment, the shade of a red apricot blossom.

From then on, Ganno spent every evening painting the canvas of his toenails with pine needles.

"You're gonna lose it all in the inspection next week, you know," Jiji told the man busy at work on nail art that didn't even look good on him, sounding exasperated.

"That's why I have to hurry," Ganno replied happily. "I'm almost at the baby toe."

High treason, a minimum of seventeen years. Ganno's crime had been painting a portrait of a noble confronting the prime minister. His father had also been a painter, and he'd had a brush in his hand ever since he could remember, never given the choice not to pick one up.

Ganno was painting a picture in a week with paint that had taken him two weeks to make. Sasuke understood Ganno's dedication and desire to finish this painting, even though he knew he'd have to erase it the following week. Games and goals were critical in this place.

As a general rule prisoners shared cells that were six tatami mats large. Putting that many adults in such a small space was bound to lead to clashes, and men regularly beat each other bloody or bullied one cellmate until they grew weak and died. The cell Sasuke was in, however, was relatively peaceful. None of the men in it were bosom buddies, but they didn't have any real conflicts.

Ganno was immersed in his artistic activities, while Jiji and Penzila oscillated between hope and despair with every roll of the dice. Sasuke stared absently at the moon until it was time for lights out. This scene played out every night in their cell.

At the end of each turn, Jiji and Penzila would take turns cajoling Sasuke to join them.

"C'mon, Sasuke! You play too."

"We'll go easy on you at first."

"No." Sasuke had just turned down yet another invitation when he heard a sound and turned his gaze toward the window.

A shadow momentarily broke the stream of pale moonlight shining on the courtyard. The guards patrolling, no doubt.

There was something that bothered Sasuke about the sentries here. And now, during their free time, was the perfect chance to investigate.

"I changed my mind." He stood up and sat down again in front of Penzila. "I'll play you."

"Huh?" Penzila stared at him. "For real? All right!"

"I don't have any cigarettes. Can I bet this instead?" Sasuke put his hand in his pocket and pretended to pull something out, while he worked his chakra at his fingertips. Applying an Earth Style jutsu, he raised the ratio of a specific element included in the soil to the maximum possible, arranged the atoms on the diagonal, and made it crystallize like that.

A red stone rolled into his hand. An enormous ruby, about the size of a cherry.

"Huh? A gem? Is it real?"

"No way. It's gotta be glass."

Penzila and Jiji stared hard at the gem.

Sasuke neither denied nor confirmed, but the jewel in the palm of his hand was indeed the real thing physically. Unfortunately, it was man-made.

"I mean, getting a pretty glass bead, well." Penzila shrugged. "Can't put a match to it and breathe it in. No way to enjoy it."

"Listen, you," Jiji snapped. "You got no more cigarettes to bet with anyway. I took them all in the game before. Wager kitchen duty or something."

"I don't want cigarettes, and we don't need to change anyone's duty shift." Sasuke picked up the teacup. "Instead, do me one favor."

"Favor?" Penzila asked.

"I'll tell you after." Sasuke set the teacup down on the tatami mat and grabbed three dice. Then he lifted his face and asked Penzila, "What's the best roll?"

"You don't even know the rules." Penzila sighed. "Ones. All three dice say one."

"Okay, then I'll roll that."

Jiji and Penzila looked at each other. Ganno also stopped his work and turned his gaze toward Sasuke.

Sasuke brought chakra up into the palm of his clenched hand, and when he tossed the dice, he sent with them a faint breeze, too slight to be noticed.

Chak! The wooden dice landed in the teacup.

Penzila gaped at the three dots there. "Seriously?"

The three dice, of course, all displayed ones, just as Sasuke had said they would.

Jiji and Ganno stared, stunned, while Sasuke stood up quietly.

"I win, right?" he said.

"That's some luck, saying you'll get ones and then actually rolling them. It's gotta be a trick," Penzila objected.

Jiji patted his shoulder. "Give it up, man."

Tricks were commonplace in the games among the prisoners. The unspoken rule in this place was no trick was a trick unless you caught the other man squarely in the act.

"You promised to do me a favor, right, Penzila?" Sasuke said.

Penzila sighed. "I'm not doing nothing too hard."

"Relax. It's a simple thing." Sasuke headed for the door. "I'm going for a walk. If the guards come around to check in, cover for me."

Penzila grinned at first, but when he realized Sasuke was serious, he lunged for the other man's legs. During their free time before lights out, they were allowed to do what they wanted provided they stayed in their cells. But even one step out of their cells, they were in violation of the rules.

"I can't! No way!" Penzila cried. "How'm I supposed to cover for you when there's clearly one person too few in here?!"

"Puff up the futons," Sasuke suggested.

"As if that'll fool them! The guards aren't five years old, you know!" Penzila squealed.

Sasuke stepped into the hallway.

"Sasuke!" Jiji called through the bars. "You know what you're in for here? They find out you broke the rules, it's straight to the Box for you. And your excuses'll be useless up against Meno. He'll devour you."

"I'll be back soon," Sasuke replied evenly.

"That's not the problem here," Penzila groaned.

There were two buildings on the observatory premises, east and west, with a courtyard separating them. The west side was the residential structure where the prisoners slept, a barracks that looked like it had been built in about five minutes with whatever twigs there were in the area.

The east side was the main observatory building. Prisoners were not permitted inside, but Sasuke boldly walked right through the front door.

When he set foot inside, he was welcomed by a plush rug. The main building was the complete opposite of the prisoners' residence. It was a magnificent brick structure like an imperial palace, a renovated building from the Tatar era. With four stories above ground, it was large for the standard in this country.

Although the prisoners wept themselves to sleep on a hard stone floor, wrapped in threadbare blankets, the main building had plush rugs not just in every room, but even on the floors of the hallways and staircases. With walls sturdily constructed of bricks fixed in place with mortar, it was free of drafts, and the guards' rooms even boasted large fireplaces. It was an entirely different world from the residence, where icicles would form in the cells when it snowed.

Sasuke walked down the hallways, hiding in rooms or plastering himself to the ceiling to avoid the guards who happened along. He didn't erase his aura in order to draw the large lizard, Meno, to him. Although he couldn't interrogate an animal with words, he could likely gain some information from Meno by using genjutsu to control him.

Everything about Meno—reflexes, speed, strength—far surpassed the abilities of any ordinary lizard. In all likelihood he was a summoned creature. Given that he was loyal to the director, there was a good chance that the summoner was Zansul. This country had never had ninja of its own, but Sasuke had been told the prime minister was collecting rogue shinobi for war.

If Zansul was a shinobi and using a summoning technique to manifest Meno, then the two of them would have been connected by chakra.

But he had questions about the lengthy period of Meno's summoning. He was always ambling around the observatory and watching over the prisoners, morning and night. This meant that Zansul was summoning the creature for a minimum of twenty hours a day. That was simply too long. Either the amount of chakra Zansul possessed was vast or the mechanism was fundamentally different from the summoning technique passed down in the Land of Fire—

Tak.

He heard the sound of claws on the floor ahead in the hallway. He stopped where he was, and his gaze met a pair of yellow eyes floating in space.

Meno oozed out of the darkness to reveal himself.

"There you are." Sasuke raised his eyelids and concentrated his power in his eyes.

Sharingan.

The red eye with the three tomoe caught Meno's gaze. Instantly, Sasuke activated his ocular jutsu and pulled the lizard into the world of illusion.

That was supposed to happen, anyway.

Bang!

Meno kicked at the floor and came flying at Sasuke. The sharp claws, now bared, sliced at him and cut off a lock of his hair.

The genjutsu didn't work?

Sasuke dodged the charging lizard, but his back hit a wall and he was forced to stop. With the explosive power of a spring, Meno closed the distance between them in an instant.

Sasuke met the yellow eyes again, but the result was of course the same. The genjutsu didn't take.

He slid beneath the charging Meno, pushed up on his chest with a palm strike, and swung a leg out to sweep his feet out from under him.

Sasuke heard the sound of the floor cracking as he lay face

up beneath Meno, and he decided to abandon any further attack. It was too dangerous to leave any traces of the fight and inadvertently put the director on guard. He'd come to the main building to do this because there were fewer prying eyes, but all his efforts would have been in vain if he smashed the building up.

He pulled back, and as if to take advantage of the opening, Meno opened his eyes wide.

Waving his long tail like a whip, the beast came flying at Sasuke. When Sasuke took an easy step back to dodge it, Meno came at him in a suicide charge.

So fast!

Sasuke manifested some ice with a general Water Style technique to create an impromptu kunai and cut off the claws closing in on him, along with the toes they were attached to.

Meno kept coming at him without so much as flinching, and Sasuke sliced at his chest.

"Arngh!" Meno cried and stumbled forward. A yellowish liquid dripped from the rough wound in its stomach.

Not good.

Sasuke immediately regretted his actions, but it was too late.

Meno staggered and then raced toward a small window used for lighting, smashed through the wall, and leaped down into the courtyard. The lizard then ran off as fast as possible, leaving a trail of the yellow liquid.

Sasuke bit his lip and dropped his gaze to his hand, where the unpleasant sensation of the hit lingered.

That final flash of kunai had gone in fairly deeply. He might have dealt the creature a fatal blow.

However.

The next morning, Sasuke looked down at the courtyard from his usual seat in the cafeteria and saw a familiar long tail waving back and forth down below. He opened his eyes wide in confusion.

Ridiculous. There's no way.

Perhaps feeling his gaze on him, Meno looked back at Sasuke. But the lizard quickly turned his face away, as though he had no memory of the events of the previous evening.

Meno was alive.

Sasuke was certain he had injured it pretty seriously, and yet there wasn't a mark on it. He couldn't understand what this meant. It was almost like he was the one the ocular jutsu had been used on.

"So you were the one who dared lay a hand on Meno, hm, number four-eight-seven?" a hostile voice said suddenly from behind.

Zansul.

Sasuke had been taking a wait-and-see approach to direct contact with the man, but if he knew about the attack on Meno, then there was no point in waiting anymore. Sasuke had a few questions he'd like answered himself.

He activated his Sharingan as he looked back at the director. Eyes red, the three tomoe that floated up in his iris caught Zansul's gaze.

Sasuke gasped, very slightly.

He hadn't realized it until he looked at Zansul with the Sharingan. The eyes on the other side of Zansul's glasses were mere glass spheres.

"Glass eyes," he said slowly.

"How clever of you." Zansul narrowed his eyes, and the corners of his mouth turned up in a smile. "I'm surprised you noticed. Not one of the men I work with every day has caught on."

Zansul stretched out a hand and touched the window frame behind Sasuke. The gesture was very natural, and no one looking at him would think he couldn't see. No matter how many times Sasuke double-checked, Zansul's eyes remained unchanged. They were nothing more than glass spheres.

"It seems you can use some ninjutsu, hm? But remember this." As his false left eye spun around like it had its own mind, he brought his mouth toward Sasuke's ear and said in a whisper, "A mere shinobi can never take Meno from me."

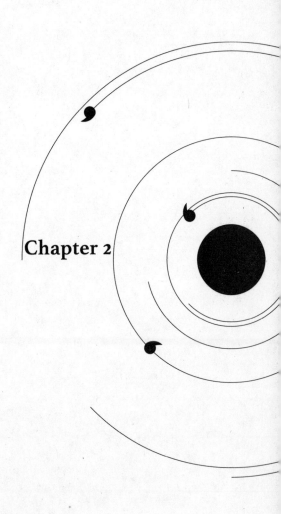

Chapter 2

The next day, the guards punished Sasuke for the first time.

The reason they gave was that he had looked away during roll call. The batons they swung with glee landed on Sasuke's shoulders, collarbone, and back in turn.

Naturally, for Sasuke, being hit by average people was of no real consequence. But even so, it hurt, and it did make him angry. He reflexively clicked his tongue in annoyance, which was taken as insubordination, and he got a few extra slaps for that.

"What's with them? Up until yesterday, they were all on eggshells around you, and now they're breaking out the truncheons," Jiji snarled as they worked, not realizing that a guard was behind him, and he too took a baton to the stomach.

And then Sasuke got three times as many blows because he hadn't warned Jiji not to chat during work.

The sentries were clearly under orders from the director to target Sasuke.

But since he hadn't been tied down or locked away in solitary, this new targeting didn't mean his identity as a ninja of Konoha had been found out. If it had, he wouldn't have been allowed to mix with the other prisoners and dig at the ground with his hoe.

Zansul likely thought Sasuke had some shinobi knowledge and was thrown in with the general population of prisoners. And that he'd toyed with his precious Meno. Sasuke was clearly a little too full of himself, he thought, and so Zansul would make him suffer.

Sasuke met the ends of batons from eight different guards that day. He wasn't working fast enough. He didn't answer when called. His eyes were defiant. He was beaten again and again, and while none of the beatings did him any real damage, the more beatings he got, the angrier he became.

At the end of the day, just as he was about to sleep, the patrol beat him, citing that his hair was too long. He seriously thought about paying them back double. If he hadn't infiltrated this place for Naruto's sake, he would have broken a rib or two.

"Sasuke, you're really catching it today, huh?"

"Those guards sure have a score to settle with you all of a sudden."

Penzila and Ganno both voiced their sympathy for Sasuke.

The guards often bullied prisoners as a way of killing time. But the ones they targeted had always been weak and timid, the type who wouldn't fight back when they were made the butt of jokes. Sasuke wasn't one of those prisoners.

"It's no big deal," Sasuke said as if he couldn't care less, but his tone conveyed his obvious annoyance.

"They're seriously riled up," Jiji retorted. "You do something to make the director mad?"

"Maybe he just hates the look of him?" Penzila said. "He looks like he'd hate anyone more handsome than him."

"Yeah. He's definitely way too proud."

While they chatted brightly, the room abruptly went dark. Lights out.

Every night at that time, the lights were turned off with no warning whatsoever and not turned on again until morning, no matter what happened. Even when the man three cells down had a heart attack, they didn't turn the lights on.

Jiji and the others groped around to find their futons and climbed into them. After a few minutes, Sasuke heard the breathing around him drop into a regular rhythm. Not only were they exhausted from the day's work, but their bodies had grown accustomed to the rhythm of the hours here.

After checking that they were all asleep, he pulled on the bars of the door and left the cell.

As Sasuke started out into the halls of the residence, he wrapped a thin piece of fabric around his wrist.

The red strip was proof that he had permission to be out of his cell. They were given out by guards when there was work to be done outside of normal hours or when a prisoner had to go to the infirmary outside of free time. As long as he was wearing it, he wouldn't be deemed to be in violation of the rules and attacked by Meno. He had nicked it from the pocket of a guard who had left it wide open as he raised his baton to strike Sasuke earlier that day.

He killed his aura as he walked down the chilly corridor and heard someone weeping.

The sound was coming from a steel cabinet that held cleaning supplies and was up against the wall. He could guess what was going on, but he couldn't exactly walk on past and ignore it.

When he opened the door, he found a skinny man with curly hair stuffed inside, hands and feet bound with hemp rope.

"Eep!" When the man saw Sasuke, his whole body stiffened.

The wrists bound in front of his chest were wet with saliva, and there were clear bite marks on them. If he cried out, Meno would find him that much faster, so he was biting his own hands to hold back his screams.

"What are you doing here?" Sasuke demanded.

"Uh. Um," the man stammered. "I was coming back from the john when one of the old hands got me. Locked me up in here…"

Bullying then.

Sasuke pulled the rope from the man's wrists and ankles.

When temperamental men were locked up in an environment like this for days on end, they looked for others to take their stress out on, and the majority of those targeted were weaker guys. Guys who had no friends to protect them. Or sickly guys with one foot in the grave anyway.

"Where's your pass?" Sasuke asked.

"Gone." The man shook his head. "They took it…"

Sasuke clicked his tongue, unwound the red fabric from his arm, and pushed it on the trembling man. If he stepped into the hallway with no pass, he'd be found by Meno and eaten sooner or later.

With servile thanks, the man ran out into the corridor, and Sasuke watched him go with genuine sympathy.

For Sasuke, this was nothing more than a place he was infiltrating temporarily. But for that man, it was a graveyard. At the current pace of work, Sasuke had no idea when the telescope would be finished, but the possibility that the man would die before it was completed was extremely high.

He wasn't good with weak people. He never knew what he should do.

Tak.

He heard the sound of hard claws hitting the floor behind him.

Wind touched the nape of his neck.

The sharp talons slashed through Sasuke's back, ripping him in two—or so it appeared. But then Meno noticed Sasuke plastered to the ceiling and snorted.

Boom!

The end of Meno's tail smashed into the ceiling. Sasuke allowed himself to drop to the floor amid the falling fragments of wood and examined Meno's belly from very close up. There was indeed nothing along the lines of an injury there. But he was sure he'd sliced open the beast's stomach the previous night.

"That's some healing ability," he remarked. "Or did you switch out with a different lizard?"

Expressionless, Meno charged at Sasuke.

A flash of claws ripped through empty air, and Meno fell forward with the force of the follow-through.

Sasuke was already dancing forward beneath him. He kicked at the maw covered with hard scales and followed up with two side kicks to the belly.

Just as he delivered the last of these blows, the long, lithe tail came flying at him from one side.

He caught the tip with his right hand and yanked hard, and Meno lost his balance and flipped over onto his stomach. Sasuke immediately grabbed his neck and tried to use his Sharingan once more, since he had nothing to lose doing so and maybe something to gain. But the result was the same. Meno did not succumb to the genjutsu.

Meno narrowed his eyes sharply, perhaps feeling humiliated at being caught under Sasuke like this. He twisted around and thrust his head forward in an attempt to rip off Sasuke's.

Sasuke leaped back, and the claw on Meno's foot grazed his cheek. His skin split, and the smallest scratch of blood emerged.

He braced himself for yet another attack and unsheathed his hidden dagger. But contrary to his expectations, Meno leaped back, away from Sasuke.

What's he doing?

Sasuke didn't let his guard down as he wondered how the lizard would attack him from that distance, but then he was assaulted by a wave of dizziness.

He staggered back, and for one brief moment, his focus shifted away from Meno.

When he came back to himself with a gasp, Meno was baring his fangs and closing in on him. Four claws shot out at him and tickled the ends of his hair when Sasuke jumped to the left and dodged the attack somehow.

When his feet hit the ground again, he was overcome with another wave of dizziness. Reeling, he braced himself and desperately tried to bring his shaking vision into focus.

He threw out a hand against the wall and dropped to his knees as Meno came at him once again.

His heart pounded hard against his ribs, and all the strength drained out of his legs.

"Hah! ...Haah..."

The inside of his chest was so hot. Meno's sharp claws glittered in his washed-out field of view.

With his free hand, Sasuke pulled out his sword and whipped it through the air. The supporting beam and floor were cut away, and the chunk of wood dropped down to the floor below.

Meno immediately gave chase, leaping into the hole after Sasuke. He swiveled his head, seeking out Sasuke.

But Sasuke's form and scent were already gone.

"Haah! Ah..."

Panting, Sasuke crept forward along the dark corridor, pressed up against the wall.

He'd managed to shake Meno off, but his body was growing number by the second.

What flashed through his mind was the moment Meno's claws grazed his cheek. He was certain that was when the poison entered his system, but he'd never heard of a lizard with poisonous claws. Zansul had likely painted the poison on them.

"Ngh... Unnh..."

He began to shiver uncontrollably.

A fierce chill ran up his spine, and his mind went blank. His skin was hot to the touch, like it was on fire. And yet the core of his body was so cold, he felt like his insides would freeze, and he couldn't stop shivering.

He worked some chakra in the palm of his hand to create some water with Water Style and brought it to his mouth. But he'd barely gotten his hand to his lips when the tips of his fingers began to shake, and he could no longer even knead chakra properly. The water spilled onto his collar and dripped down toward his waist.

"Haah... Dammit..."

His vision twisted. His ears were filled with impossibly loud auditory hallucinations as though fireworks were going off inside his head.

The situation was dire.

When it came to common poisons, his resistance was such that he could take several times the lethal dose and it would still have no effect. That this poison affected him so strongly and quickly meant that it was either extremely powerful or something unknown and particular to this region.

"Hah... Haaah..."

His breathing grew shallow and labored as if his throat were blocked, and he dragged his rebellious body forward, holding onto the wall for support.

His heart was making an awful sound and interfering with his breathing. It was like he was hyperventilating and having a heart attack at the same time.

He lapped up the remaining drops of Water Style water in his palm, but this didn't do anything to ease his pain. He leaned against the wall and wondered if he should just wait for the symptoms to subside.

Tak.

Sasuke heard the footstep echoing in the distance through the piercing pounding in his head and froze.

This was bad. Someone was coming.

If he ran into an enemy in this state, it would be the end for him.

The footsteps gradually grew closer.

Sasuke brought up the three tomoe in his eyes and desperately tried to focus his blurred vision. He wasn't sure he could make his body move the way he wanted it to anymore. Whoever was on their way down this hall, he had no choice but to rely on genjutsu to get through it.

He held his breath and waited as the footfalls grew louder.

Tak, tak, tak...

The sound of feet hitting the stone of the hall floor disappeared, and a moment later, he felt an aura immediately behind him.

His mind reacted, but his body didn't follow.

A hand stretched out from behind to cover his eyes with the Sharingan activated. A soft hand.

Sasuke gasped.

He knew the fingers covering his face.

No, don't be absurd. What would she be doing here?

Without the strength left to even turn around, Sasuke fell backwards, and a familiar warmth caught him.

"I got you, Sasuke."

It was Sakura's voice.

•

Laid on a bed in the infirmary, Sasuke took quick, shallow breaths. *Fwoo, fwoo.*

The pulse that shook his eardrums and the disturbing sensation of his inner ear canal being turned inside out had more or less gone away. When he tentatively tried to move his arms and legs, he was pleased to find that he could control them again, more or less.

His wife opened the curtain surrounding the bed on all sides and poked her face in. "How are you feeling?"

"Mm. Much better."

Sasuke sat up slowly and got out of the bed. He still felt a little dizzy, but he'd be back to his old self again before too long.

He was more concerned with why Sakura was here.

"Judging from your symptoms, I'd say it was likely a type of poison with action potential effects. It obstructs the chakra network, causes depolarization, and overexcites the central nervous system. The fact that you have no resistance to it means that the substance is particular to this region."

Sakura rolled up his sleeve. After swabbing the inside of his elbow with an alcohol-soaked cotton ball, she said, "This will pinch a little," as if talking to a child, and pushed a needle into his vein.

"Sakura." As he watched his own blood fill the tube attached to the needle, Sasuke asked slowly, "Why are you here? What about Sarada?"

"She's doing a homestay with Master Iruka," she replied. "I came to tell you about a change in the mission."

"A change in the mission?"

At present, Naruto and Nine Tails were suffering from some unknown disease. According to the tailed beast, the Sage of Six Paths had also been ill with the same symptoms. And during his stay in the Land of Redaku, he had recovered from that illness.

The details of how the Sage of Six Paths had been cured were a mystery. Therefore, it had been decided that Kakashi would infiltrate the capital of the Land of Redaku to look for clues.

But it took many long days to reach even the outer edges of the Land of Redaku. With no contact from Kakashi, Naruto's condition grew worse and worse. The majority of the seemingly relevant literature that existed in the Land of Fire was written in an ancient language, and even with a team of specialized scholars, it would be slow going to decipher them. It appeared that the Sage of Six Paths had stayed for a lengthy period at an astronomical research institute together with someone called Jean-Marc Tatar, but the scholars hadn't been able to unearth any more than that.

While they dawdled, Naruto might end up too far gone to help. Frustrated by the slow progress, Sasuke had ignored the voices trying to stop him and set out for the Tatar Observatory on his own in search of clues related to the Sage of Six Paths' illness.

And after he had left the Land of Fire, Sakura came chasing after him.

"While I was on my way, Shikamaru's hawk brought me this," Sakura said, holding out a folded piece of paper covered with Shikamaru's familiar handwriting. "He said there's something about the Sage of Six Paths' illness in this book that Master Kakashi found in the capital. This is a copy of that section."

Wasting away from a curious illness, the Sage of Six Paths had cause to attend the Land of Redaku and thus did meet the astronomer Tatar on his path.

Ministered to by this Tatar, his illness nonetheless troubled him yet.

One evening, Tatar espied a meteor approaching the land. The Sage of Six Paths caught this fallen meteorite in hand and split it in twain in a singular motion.

A bright light spilled forth from the halved meteorite to bathe the Sage of Six Paths. Instantly, the Sage was freed of his illness of many years.

The meteor which fell from the heavens presented him with blessed strength, allowing his chakra to expand without limit. Tatar named the substance in the meteor that was the source of his power "ultra particles."

To stop those who would struggle for this grand power he held, he hid half of these ultra particles in "the sky that fell to the earth," and the other half in "the star that never strays."

The ultra particles sleep in this world well protected by a path lined with stars.

Should others be consumed with the illness of the Sage of Six Paths, they are destined to desire the power of the ultra particles. And thus this distant power will be made to come to this distant land.

Any who would seek out this state must tarry in the Land of Redaku reveling with the Map of the Heavens.

"Should others be consumed with the illness of the Sage of Six Paths, hm?" Sasuke said, rereading the last three lines.

These ultra particles were the key to curing Naruto's illness.

According to this text, the Sage of Six Paths split them into two and hid one group in "the sky that fell to the earth" and the other in "the star that never strays."

"This is just a hypothesis, but Shikamaru and I both think that Naruto's illness is probably some kind of malfunction in his chakra channels that happened because he took a tailed beast into his body. And if the substance this meteor contained—what Tatar called ultra particles—has the power to heal those symptoms—"

"We have to find it," Sasuke said in a tone that brooked no argument, and Sakura nodded.

"Which is why the new mission is to look for this 'Map of the Heavens' and obtain the ultra particles," she said. "First up, figuring out what exactly this map is. A book? A painting? Something else?"

"I understand the change in the mission. But that isn't reason for you to be here." Sasuke glared at her.

"I'm a shinobi too, after all." Sakura furrowed her brow. "I leave the village when I have to."

"You shouldn't deliberately court danger. You could easily have sent a hawk with the message."

"I did. But it didn't make it. The hawk came back with the letter still attached."

"What?" Now it was Sasuke's turn to furrow his brow.

Birds caught in the wild might have failed in a mission like this, but it was rare for a hawk raised and trained in the village from the time it was a chick to fail to deliver a letter.

"I don't know why," Sakura said. "But this is time sensitive, so I decided to infiltrate the place as a doctor and simply tell you myself. And now that I'm here, I can help you."

"No need. Go back. It's too dangerous."

"Dangerous?" Sakura got a very serious look on her face. "You think I can't handle it?"

"I know your strength and abilities. But I'm telling you that I can handle this by myself," he replied. "And something's going on behind the scenes at this institute. Ocular jutsu doesn't work on the director or on Meno."

"Then all the more reason I should stay," she insisted. "You need a partner on special missions that can't be handled with brute force, right?"

What Sakura said made sense.

When it came to battle, Sasuke boasted a strength unmatched by anyone other than the Seventh Hokage. But he had to admit, this undercover mission was closer to espionage. In situations where a show of force simply would not work—like extracting information from someone immune to ocular jutsu or taking care of the job without hurting anyone or being found out—having a co-conspirator was a significant advantage.

"Plus, the environment here is awful," Sakura continued.

"People are dropping like flies from malnutrition and overwork, and yet no one thinks this is a problem. I proposed some improvements to Director Zansul, but it was like he didn't even hear me. He said he can bring in fresh recruits soon enough, no matter how many people die. He and the guards think you and the other prisoners are nothing more than easily replaceable labor."

"I thought I told you not to do anything dangerous," he said. "What would you have done if you'd upset the director and he started paying real attention to you?"

"I'm a doctor. I have a duty to do whatever I can for the health of everyone in this place." When it came to her work, Sakura was extremely stubborn.

They glared at each other for a moment, but it was Sasuke who gave in with a sigh.

"Fine. Do what you want. But don't put yourself in danger."

"I would never." She smiled and whirled around toward her desk. "Okay then. I'll send a sample of your blood to Konoha. And a situation report to Master Kakashi, just in case."

He frowned. "I thought hawks wouldn't work as a means of communication."

"Watch." Sakura whistled, and a small hawk came flying out of the back room. The strip of fabric the prisoners wore when they were out after hours was tied neatly around its neck like a little red scarf. "I think the other hawk came back to Konoha because Meno chased it away. The ironclad rule here is no unauthorized personnel allowed. But with this scrap of fabric, it might not be seen as an intruder."

"Makes sense." Sasuke nodded.

Someone knocked on the door of the infirmary.

Office hours had long passed. Husband and wife exchanged a look, wondering who would be here at this hour.

"Doctor, are you still awake?"

It was Jiji. Rather than his usual blustery tone, the question trailed upward, somehow soft.

Sakura gave Sasuke's shoulders a push, and he returned to the bed. The partitioning curtain was yanked shut before his eyes, and he heard the sound of Jiji drawing near.

"Hey, Doc? You in here?"

Realizing that his feet were visible beneath the curtain, Sasuke raised his legs onto the bed, shoes and all. At the same time, Jiji's silhouette fell on the partition.

"Oh, huh. You are here."

"Jiji, what's wrong?" Sakura asked calmly. "It's late."

"Take a look at this. Working yesterday, I burst a blister. I told the guard it hurt so bad, I couldn't sleep, and he gave me permission to come here."

"Sit down there. What's your number again?"

"Five-four-four."

Sasuke heard the sound of pen on paper. Sakura was probably creating a chart for Jiji.

The treatment wouldn't take long. He sat cross-legged on the bed and decided to wait until Jiji left.

"Doc, you got any cigarettes? That's the best thing for stopping pain."

"Of course I don't. What do you think a doctor's office is?"

"I'll do anything if you give me a cigarette. You really don't got any? Your old butts'd be just fine."

"This will sting. I'm going to disinfect the wound."

Sakura took Jiji's arm and rolled up his sleeve slowly. Sasuke couldn't see it, but he could tell from the movement of the shadows on the curtain.

He could tell just by listening to Jiji that his bit about being in too much pain to sleep was nothing more than a pretext. His cellmate had come here with some ulterior motive. That much was obvious.

Separated from Sasuke by nothing more than a curtain, Jiji

moved from topic to topic—he wanted a painkiller, he felt like he had a fever—and Sakura evaded his conversational tactics as necessary to continue treating him.

"Hey, Doc? You're not from around here, yeah?"

"What makes you think that?"

"Your name, color of your hair. I mean, cherry pink hair, I never seen that before. It's pretty, huh?"

Sasuke saw Jiji's hand move to touch Sakura's hair and couldn't stand it any longer. He grabbed Jiji's wrist from behind.

Sakura rolled her eyes.

"Huh?" Jiji's eyes grew round like saucers at the sudden appearance of his cellmate. "Sasuke? Wait. What are you doing here?"

"I could ask you the same thing," Sasuke said coolly.

"I came to get this blister patched up. It burst, and it's been really hurting me. The bleeding's stopped, but it still smarts."

A lie.

"You'll be in trouble if it gets infected. Take this." Sakura held a small cup filled with a green liquid toward Jiji.

"What is it?" he asked.

"The extract of medicinal plants. It has an antibacterial effect."

"Whoa! Smells like garbage! If I'm gonna drink something antibacterial, I'd rather it be saké."

"About your earlier question," Sasuke said. "The doctor there is my wife."

Jiji spat out a mouthful of green liquid. Wiping away what dripped down his chin, he looked bewildered as he looked back and forth between Sasuke and Sakura.

"For real? Your wife? Huh? Does that mean you're married to the doctor? Seriously? Huh? You're married?!"

"I never said a word about being single," Sasuke noted.

"No, but a guy like you, he's usually single," Jiji replied.

What kind of judgement is that?

"And like, what's your wife doing doctoring all the way out here?"

"I came to see Sasuke," Sakura lied nonchalantly. "Unlike prison, there's no visiting system here. But I just had to see him, so I decided to get hired on as a doctor."

"Huh, that so?" Jiji readily accepted her story, and Sasuke turned a shocked gaze on him.

"You're not surprised?"

"Why would I be surprised?" Jiji looked at Sasuke curiously. "It's just normal behavior. I mean, a married couple, they're always together and all."

"Jiji. Don't tell anyone that Sakura's my wife," Sasuke told Jiji as they walked down the long hallway after leaving the infirmary. On his wrist was the strip of fabric Sakura had given him.

"Gotcha." Jiji winked. "If anyone finds out she's family with a prisoner, the doc'll have to leave. But I never dreamed you were married, Sasuke. You gotta tell a fellow important stuff like that."

"You never asked," Sasuke reminded him.

"No, no. We definitely had adjacent conversations. I'm sure of that."

Cellmates were basically in constant contact, so they ended up covering pretty much every topic of conversation. Naturally, girlfriends and marriages came up any number of times, but being undercover, Sasuke had always avoided going too deep into that one.

"Jiji. You've got a fiancée, don't you?" Sasuke said.

"Yup." Jiji grinned. "She's working in the capital right now. Once I've done my time, we're getting hitched."

Sasuke dropped his gaze to his feet. The dyed rug was pale in the light of the moon pouring in through the large window.

I mean, a married couple, they're always together and all.

Sasuke had more or less digested Jiji's words. But they didn't really click for him, given that he was often away from the village on long-term missions.

"Do you think that married couples should be together?" he asked.

"Well, of course." Jiji's response was instantaneous. "I mean, the doc wanted to be with you, so she went and got herself hired by this prison way out in the middle of nowhere."

"Oh, I don't know about that," Sasuke said. "Although it's true I tend to be away from home."

"Away from home?" Jiji asked. "How much we talking here?"

"There've been periods when I haven't gone home for several years."

"You serious?!" Jiji was stunned. "Years? I mean, that length of time, you couldn't really say anything if she just assumed the two of you were done."

Sasuke cocked his head to one side. "Why would she assume that?"

"Why wouldn't she?" Jiji stared back at him just as seriously.

"It's not as though I left her behind without telling her," Sasuke said. "They need Sakura back home, and I have to work outside the country. That's just how it is. Nothing more than that. We exchange letters."

"No, but still. You wouldn't hate it if some bad apple like me came along while you were gone? You don't wear rings in your country?" Jiji looked at Sasuke with an honestly worried expression on his face. "I mean, a married couple, they're always together and all."

Sasuke couldn't really understand what Jiji was trying to say.

Sakura was family. He was certain that no matter where he went, that would never change. He'd never heard of anyone not being family anymore when they were separated by however many kilometers. Even when he had had that deep hatred of

Itachi in his heart, the fact that Itachi was his older brother never changed.

To Sasuke, Sakura was family and a partner to live his life with. Even if they weren't connected by blood, even if they couldn't see each other every day, that fact would always remain.

That was his thinking on the matter, but going to the trouble of putting it into words and communicating it to Jiji was annoying and didn't suit his personality. So he simply nodded and said, "I see," before changing the subject.

"Have you ever heard anything about a Map of the Heavens?"

"Map of the Heavens?" Jiji repeated, his voice trailing upward as he cocked his head to one side. "Nope, never heard of it. From the name, I'd guess it was some astronomy book. Maybe it's in the library? Try asking Penzila."

"Why Penzila?" Sasuke asked, and Jiji blinked at him in surprise. "Huh? I mean, he's the library attendant."

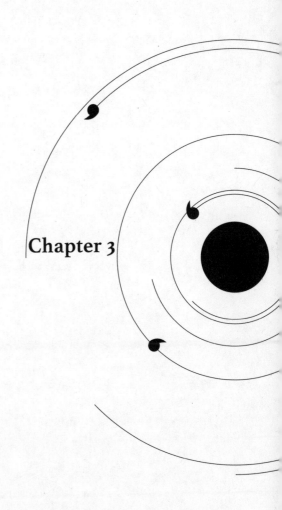

Chapter 3

Sasuke cut across the courtyard under the orange-red light of the setting sun and headed for the library that sat neatly in front of the main building. The only time prisoners were allowed to use the library was before and after supper, and only briefly.

When he opened the rusted brass door, he found rows of shoulder-height bookcases. The building housed many parchment texts that were fragile and quick to discolor, and the facility was constructed of sandstone and laterite, which was even more drafty than the prisoner residence. In other words, it was cold. And gloomy. The sole light source was a line of small windows which served more for the purpose of ventilation than lighting, and the sunlight that came through these tiny squares fell to the floor at regular intervals.

He had assumed the place would be deserted, but he saw prisoners sitting on the floor scattered here and there, flipping through the pages of books. A large majority of them couldn't read, but they enjoyed looking at the pictures.

Just as they'd discussed when they met earlier, Sakura was in front of a bookshelf on the south side of the room. Even when

Sasuke approached, she kept her eyes firmly focused on the stacks, pretending to be searching for a book.

After Sasuke had wandered through the stacks for an appropriate amount of time, he came to stand on the opposite side of the shelf Sakura was browsing. There was no one else around.

"The librarian is my cellmate," he said, hiding his mouth with the cover of a book.

There was a brief silence, and then a response came from the other side of the shelves before him.

"The one with his head on the table, napping? Tall, skinny. Short hair."

"He likes to gamble. If you offer to play him, he'll definitely accept. I'll talk to him first. You come along after and make your move."

"Roger."

Sakura closed the book in her hands with a loud *clap*. Taking this as a signal, Sasuke approached the man napping with a book over his face and slapped his shoulder.

"Penzila."

"Ah! You scared me!" Penzila jumped up and opened his eyes. "Sasuke? Weird to see you here."

"I could say the same," Sasuke told him. "I never dreamed you'd take the librarian job. It's so much work."

"I asked for the job. Gotta show how I'm a model prisoner, set my sights on getting out on parole. Unlike you lot, my term's a short one."

"If you're a model prisoner, then maybe treat the books with a little more respect?" Sasuke suggested.

The book under Penzila's face was no doubt valuable, but its open pages were now dotted with saliva.

"Ah! Crap!" He rubbed at the spots with the edge of his sleeve, and the page ripped. "Aaah, I tore Kubinaga's face."

"Kubinaga?"

"The big guy here." Penzila pointed at a picture of a creature with a long neck. The caption next to the picture read "Titan." Between Penzila's spit and the image of a now-torn face, it was hard to tell for sure, but it looked enormous relative to the trees in the background. "There's loads of dragons in this book. Even if you can't read the words, it's pretty interesting just to look at."

Sasuke quickly perused the descriptive text.

Titan: A large dragon with a long neck and tail. Total body length of nearly 100 feet. Fossils of the creature have been discovered in the area around the Tatar Observatory.

Sasuke didn't know too much about it himself, but among scholars, there was consensus that enormous creatures known as dragons had existed in this region at some point in the past. He was pretty sure they were called dinosaurs in some areas.

Before the earth's crust bulged up and created the mountains, this region had been flat wetlands, and a great number of dragons had roamed here.

"You read dragon books too?" Penzila asked. "You want me to get you my favorites?"

"No." Sasuke shook his head. "I'm actually looking for a book called *Map of the Heavens.*"

"*Map of the Heavens*?" Penzila stared back at him blankly. "Never heard of that one. If I checked the catalogue of books, I could find out. But I'll have to find a guy who can read first."

"I can read."

"Seriously?! Sasuke, you're something else!"

Sincerely impressed, Penzila pulled the library catalogue out from beneath the counter. The pile of pages, corners all turned up, was as thick as an encyclopedia, and the silk cords that bound it were worn and on the verge of snapping. Sasuke opened it carefully to find handwritten characters scrawled like snakes. There was no order at all to the list, just a random collection of titles, but he quickly found the title he was looking for.

Map of the Heavens was listed on the very first page as a critical text.

"Basement stack…'I-twenty-four.'" He read out the location of the book, and Penzila slumped his shoulders apologetically.

"Aah, the basement stacks?" he said. "You're out of luck then. Downstairs is where they keep all the super important books. The books down there are worth a hundred—a thousand times what we are. We're totally not allowed to touch them. You even go down those stairs, and you're looking at one thing and one thing only—the ultimate punishment. No ifs, ands, or buts."

The ultimate punishment—in other words, death by hanging.

"Oh? That's too bad." Sasuke frowned.

"Now you've got me curious," Sakura said from behind, acting like she just happened to be walking by.

"Oh, the doctor from the infirmary," Penzila said.

"I might be a bit interested in this *Map of the Heavens* book," she remarked. "I mean, I did come all the way out to an astronomical observatory. I was hoping to get a chance to study the stars a little."

"If you want to read about stars, we got plenty of other books," Penzila told her. "Unfortunately, this *Map of the Heavens*'s off-limits."

"Okay." Sakura grinned. "I'll read it in secret in the middle of the night. Lend me the key."

Penzila looked stunned.

"I mean, a banned book? Now I *have* to read it. It's sort of thrilling, you know? Maybe it's about how a meteor's going to come crashing to earth one of these days or something."

Penzila waved a hand back and forth. "You might be the doctor, but I can't give you the key. I'd end up hanged too."

"Then how about we play for it?" Sakura said innocently.

Penzila's face changed slightly when he heard the word "play."

"Cee-lo, cards, whatever your game is," she continued. "If I win, you give me the key to the basement."

"Hold on." Penzila frowned. "If anyone finds out you walked off with the key, I'll..."

"The guards almost never come here, right? I'll sneak in and read it at night, and then I'll give you the key back as soon as I'm done. Please!" Sakura begged and clapped her hands together pleadingly.

"Aah." Penzila looked troubled and walked nervously in circles. "I don't know."

But eventually he stopped and announced calmly, "Fine. We'll play for it."

"Yes! What'll we play?"

"Not Cee-lo. Sasuke just beat the pants off of me. I've got no luck there." Penzila shook his head. "We'll play Star Lines."

"Star Lines?"

Sakura and Sasuke both raised eyebrows in surprise at the same time. They'd never heard of the game.

"It's a game we play here. I'll go get it."

While Penzila slipped toward a bookcase further back, Sasuke said to Sakura, "You only have to pretend you're playing him. As soon as the game starts, I'll cast genjutsu on him."

"You can't do that," she said. "That's cheating."

He stared at her, dumbfounded. "Is this really the time for that?"

"I'll be fine. I wasn't Lady Tsunade's top apprentice for nothing."

Isn't Tsunade so bad at gambling it practically killed her, though?

Sakura was full of confidence, unmoved by Sasuke's concern. She took off her white doctor's coat, pushed it on Sasuke, rolled up her sleeves, and said, "Oh yeeeah!"

He wasn't sure about this, but she seemed ready to tackle the world.

While Sasuke wondered how he could convince her to do it his way, Penzila returned with a magnificent box inlaid with gold. He removed the lid to reveal picture cards that were slightly smaller than playing cards. In contrast with the size of the box, the cards were very small.

"Okay, this is Star Lines. Basically, there's twelve kinds of cards and you use them to make different kinds of hands." Penzila sat down cross-legged in front of the box and began laying out the cards. "Some guys found it a few months ago when they were cleaning up the shelves. Complete with a list of rules."

There were twelve different pictures on each of the twelve types of cards:

A white horse swimming in the ocean.

A cat staring at a lantern flame.

An orange watchfire in an iron basket.

A monkey drawing on the ground with a tree branch.

A shepherd looking up at the night sky through a glass bead.

A cow peering into a pot.

A tree trunk with sap oozing down the side.

A giant being born from the earth.

A turtle climbing a rocky mountain.

An elderly person with white hair and a cane.

A tanuki parent and child playing on a dune.

And a frog and a slug crawling across a bog.

The motifs were all over the place—human, animal, plant— painted in vivid color with what appeared to be natural mineral pigments. The picture on the back of the cards was the same: a lizard coiled around a rock. The lizard was reminiscent of Meno; was there some kind of connection there?

"There are twelve kinds of picture cards. Five of each, so sixty cards in total. We each get dealt six. And then we toss cards and take new ones like poker to form a hand. This is the list of hands. The ink's faded there, and the parts you can't read, well, just ignore them."

He held out a scrap of paper with a list of combinations that comprised the various hands.

The strongest hand, Star, was white horse, shepherd, cat, watchfire, giant, and turtle...apparently. There were traces of something written on the line beneath it, but the ink was smudged, and it was no longer legible.

Second to Star was the hand Earth, made up of cat, watchfire, tanuki, frog and slug, turtle, and old person.

There were a number of other hands, such as Twilight, Flame, Clear Sky, and New Leaf, in addition to Star and Earth, but unlike poker, there appeared to be no regularity to the combinations for the different hands. It would take a beginner player quite a bit of time to remember all the different hands. However...

"Oh, I get it. Okay. Shall we play?" Sakura said and handed the paper back to Penzila.

He frowned. "Weren't you listening, Doc? I told you, this game's all about getting the right hand. A newbie needs to have this paper out where they can see it and check the hands. Otherwise—"

"I memorized them."

"Huh?"

Sakura sat on her knees in front of Penzila, tucked her cherry-pink hair behind her ear, and straightened her back. Her cat-like almond eyes narrowed, and she stared at Penzila, like she was issuing him a challenge.

"Let's play."

This isn't what the doc's usually like, huh?

Penzila chuckled to himself when he saw the expression on Sakura's face change. He'd seen moods and personalities shift abruptly many times when people sat down to gamble. Speaking from experience, that sort of person wasn't particularly suited to games of chance. The ironclad rule when it came to gambling was not to wear your emotions on your face.

"I'm sitting in the low seat, so it's my job to deal the cards, right?" Sakura said as she picked up the deck.

"Mm hmm. From the second round on, the loser deals. But I guess this is just a one-shot, so that doesn't matter." Penzila carefully watched Sakura cut the cards with the precision he'd expect of a doctor.

Doctor Sakura was basically the only person who treated the prisoners with humanity. She'd only just arrived at the observatory, but she was already revered by many of the prisoners. She attempted to hospitalize guys who'd been beaten by their cellmates and sent a request for indoor work for a guy with arthritis who couldn't hold a hoe anymore. So far, these requests had been roundly rejected by the director, but Sakura's mere effort to provide the prisoners with care was more aid than they had gotten before she arrived at the observatory.

At the moment, however, the expression of the woman before him was different from the doctor he knew.

Penzila picked up the cards Sakura slid across the floor to him one at a time and took a look.

Not a bad group. Among the six cards, he had an old person, a cat, and a turtle. If he could pick up a watchfire, a tanuki, and a frog and slug in the next five turns, he'd have the second strongest hand, Earth.

When he glanced up, Sakura was smiling slightly as she checked her cards. "I'm sure a lot of people who like to gamble are pretty smart, hm?"

"The same as with doctors, I guess." Penzila discarded the three cards that were not old person, cat, or turtle, and drew three new ones from the deck. A second turtle, a cow, and a watchfire. Looking good. In addition to picking up a pair of turtles, he was also closer to an Earth.

Next was Sakura's turn. She tossed one card and took one from the pile. And then after a moment of hesitation, she discarded another one and drew a new one.

Second turn, third turn...

Before he knew it, the prisoners in the library had started to gather around them. They leaned forward and watched the two play with great interest.

And then it was the final turn.

Penzila hesitated. Right now, he held two turtles, an old person, a cat, a watchfire, and a frog and slug. If he discarded a turtle and drew a tanuki, he'd have Earth. But that option also meant ruining the only thing he currently had in his hand, the pair of turtles. If he drew a card that wasn't in his hand, he would have absolutely nothing all at once.

Now what to do...

Penzila glared at his cards.

His opponent was a beginner. She'd only just learned the rules. It was unlikely that she'd memorized the combinations for complicated hands like Star or Earth, equally unlikely that she was trying to pick up one of those hands. She'd probably come at him with a simple combination, like a pair or three of a kind.

In which case, maybe he should try discarding everything except his turtles. If he drew another turtle, that'd be three of a kind. Even if he didn't get a turtle, if he could draw two of the same card, that'd be two pairs.

No reason to overreach and try for Earth. The right choice was to play defensively.

Having made this decision, he was about to throw away four cards, when he suddenly met Sakura's eyes.

"Think it over as long as you want," she said gently, tilting her head to one side.

He felt like she was taking him for a fool. He snapped.

Change of strategy. I'm not getting some wishy-washy win with three of a kind or two pairs. I'm getting Earth, and I will make her weep.

He discarded half of his hard-won turtle pair and drew a card from the deck. If it was a tanuki, he'd have his Earth hand.

But if it was any other card he didn't have already, he'd end up with nothing.

When he saw the picture on the card he'd drawn, Penzila nearly leaped up into the air.

Yes!

Depicted in smudged ink was a tanuki parent and child playing on a dune. He'd gotten the second strongest hand, Earth.

"I don't need to discard." It seemed that Sakura had also completed her hand.

And thus, all five rounds were over.

Time for the showdown. The moment of decision when they laid their hands out to show each other.

"Hey, Doc, don't cry, okay?" he said, in high spirits, and neatly spread out his cards.

The gallery of onlookers crowded around them looked at the pictures on each of the six cards. The man who first realized Penzila had gotten Earth whistled.

"Earth, right out of the gate," he said, impressed.

"Is that a good hand?" Sasuke asked, and the man bobbed his head up and down.

"Second strongest hand there is. The only way you can beat that is to get Star, the strongest hand. But some of the cards in Star, you also need for Earth. Now that Penzila's gotten Earth, it's unlikely that the doctor has a Star hand."

Meaning Sakura had lost?

Sasuke stared at his wife, who kept her poker face right up to the end.

Her fingers turned a card: tanuki.

Sasuke heard several sighs from the gallery. There was no tanuki in a Star hand. Sakura had lost the game.

Which wasn't really a surprise. The game was about chance, after all. Sasuke decided he would use genjutsu on everyone in the place and pilfer the book while they were under. A red light started to bleed into his eyes.

Sakura grinned, and her pale fingers flipped over the remaining five cards: turtle, old person, cat, watchfire, and frog and slug. This combination was...

"Earth!" someone in the gallery cried with a gasp.

The two rows of cards on the floor were identical. Sakura had the same Earth hand as Penzila. In other words, the game was a draw. But Earth hardly ever came up. Was it even possible for both players to get that hand in the same round?

"It's a trick," Penzila muttered.

"Oh my! Well then, did you want to pat me down or something?" Sakura spread her arms out and held her wrists forward, with a softness that made it hard to figure out what she was up to. Her cherry-pink hair spilled forward, brushing her cheeks, and she stared at Penzila challengingly with her blue-green eyes.

Penzila fell silent, at a loss for words.

When it came to cheating, turn a blind eye unless you catch the cheater in the act—that was the rule in this place.

Half an hour since they'd started playing.

Penzila's back was damp with sweat.

Behind the six cards fanned in his hands, eyes lined with cherry-pink lashes stared back at him. When it looked like he might actually meet those eyes, he automatically lowered his gaze, and the sweat on his forehead dripped down onto his cards.

The results so far: five games, zero wins, zero losses. A draw every single time. Sakura had gone second in each round and had gotten the exact same hand as he had five times in a row.

It was impossible. She *had* to have been cheating. There was no other explanation for it.

He stared, hyper focused, each time she touched the cards, but he caught sight of absolutely nothing suspicious. And if she was manipulating the cards somehow, why would she not just go ahead and take the win? Why would she bring it to a draw every time?

"Okay, showdown. You first," Sakura said, her voice clear and crisp.

Please, let this time finally decide it.

Praying, Penzila spread his cards out.

Old person, shepherd, tanuki, tanuki, turtle, turtle. A combination of two pairs of animals was called a "tier." This was slightly better than two pairs, but he no longer cared about the strength of his hand. If it meant it would settle this contest, he'd be happy with anything.

"Another draw. What a coincidence, hm?" Sakura smiled knowingly and spread her cards out before her.

The strength abruptly drained from Penzila's body.

Old person, shepherd, tanuki, tanuki, turtle, turtle. The six cards she laid out were exactly the same combination as Penzila's. It was like looking in a mirror. Again.

"A draw." Penzila sighed.

"This is such an incredible coincidence. We're totally on the same wavelength, hm?"

That made six draws.

Sakura tapped the deck of cards against the floor to square them up. "You want to go again?" she asked as she shuffled, a slight smile on her face.

"No. I lose," Penzila declared abruptly and stood up.

I can keep playing, but it's just going to be the same every time. I can't beat this woman. And I can't lose to her. All I can do is have the life drained out of me, bit by bit, like a dog strangled slowly with a silk cord.

"Hang on," he said, slipped behind the bookcases, grabbed a brass key, and popped back out. "Here. The master key to the basement stacks. Bring it right back when you're done. If they find out it's gone, all the library clerks will get the ultimate punishment."

"I'll definitely bring it back. Thanks."

Sakura went to take the key, but Penzila yanked it up out of her reach.

"I'll just say this," he added. "Even if the title's in the catalogue, that doesn't necessarily mean that this *Heavens* or whatever it is is actually down there."

"What do you mean?" Sakura frowned. "Isn't that catalogue a collection of all the books in the library?"

"It is, but that still doesn't mean we actually have it," he told her. "You probably know this library was stored at the palace while they were fixing up the observatory. And a fair number of books went missing from it while it was there."

Why didn't you say that from the start? Sasuke glared at him.

Penzila shrugged, perhaps misinterpreting the reason for Sasuke's cold eyes on him. "Pretty awful, huh? That lot at the palace, I guess they didn't know how valuable the books were. And a dozen or so years ago, some envoy or something from somewhere made off with some pretty specific books. Story is, they never returned a single one of them."

"Specific books? Which ones?" Sakura asked.

"You know that Sage of Six Paths from the old stories?" Penzila replied. "Books of forbidden jutsu from back when he was still walking around. Should've been treasures that never left the gates, but the old king was a friendly guy, so he just let them borrow whatever they wanted. The envoy had a weird name too. I'm pretty sure it was something like Orochimaru."

Upon the unexpected mention of Orochimaru's name, Sasuke and Sakura exchanged a look. Of course, it could be someone who also had this name, but they were pretty certain this was *the* Orochimaru. That snake man always turned up where he was least expected, so it wouldn't have been at all strange if he had known about this country so distant from the Land of Fire.

But if that were the case, then what on earth drove him to come all the way to far-off Redaku?

That night, Sasuke waited for Jiji and the others to fall asleep before sneaking out of his cell and going out into the courtyard. He met up with Sakura in front of the library.

"You brought the key?" he asked, and Sakura held the bit of dull metal up next to her face.

"Of course."

They were going into the basement to retrieve *Map of the Heavens*. He hoped it wouldn't be too difficult to find.

They pushed open the tarnished brass door and went inside. When Sasuke closed the door behind them, darkness blanketed the room. There were no lamps in the library. Both shinobi called up Fire Style flames in their palms and relied on this light to move further in.

"Hey, is Jiji actually sleeping at night?" Sakura asked abruptly.

"He was sound asleep when I left the cell," Sasuke told her. "Why do you ask?"

"Lately, he's been coming to the infirmary a lot. His head hurts, his stomach hurts, all kinds of excuses. When I examine him, I can't find anything wrong. I think he just wants an excuse to skip out of work, but I'm still a bit worried."

"Probably just faking. He's the picture of health."

Sasuke felt something flutter in his stomach.

Jiji might have been Jiji, but still, there was no way he would touch Sakura, not knowing that she was Sasuke's wife. He wouldn't. At least that's what Sasuke wanted to believe.

You wouldn't hate it if some bad apple like me came along while you were gone?

Jiji's words came back to life in his ears, sounding ominous, and Sasuke froze in place.

"Hm? What's wrong?" Sakura stopped and looked at him, mystified.

He looked at her without a word and grabbed her hand. He touched the base of her ring finger and worked his chakra there. The chakra transformed into sand and slid around Sakura's finger like a ring of Saturn. *Tink!* In the blink of an eye, the ring turned from sand to silver.

"Wear this," Sasuke said grumpily as he released her hand.

"This..." She spread her fingers out in front of her and stared, baffled by the ring that had suddenly appeared on her finger.

The silver circle sparkled in the faint light, a large red gem set in the center of it. A ruby. Both silver and ruby had been generated by increasing the purity of substances in Earth Style to almost the maximum. Sasuke had used ninjutsu to create an impromptu ring.

A ring on the fourth finger of the left hand, that means you're married.

"Thanks," Sakura said shyly.

Sasuke appeared not to hear her. He self-consciously turned his back on her and began to walk.

Trailing after him, Sakura pressed the palms of her hands to her now-hot cheeks. The ring was a little crooked, but even so, it was beautiful, shining more clearly than a star or flowing water. The purity and clarity of the ruby, likely far superior to those of any naturally produced gem, was a gift of Sasuke's impressive chakra control.

Is he maybe jealous?

She knew he would only become more taciturn if she asked him, so she decided to lock it away in her heart.

She narrowed her eyes in an embarrassed smile as she stared at the red stone decorating her ring finger.

After proceeding in silence in the darkness, they came to the door at the far side of the library. When Sakura pushed the key into the hole below the handle, the spring inside lifted with a *click* and the lock opened.

"How did you win?" Sasuke asked awkwardly as he pushed the door inward.

"Oh. That. Well…" Caught staring at the ring on her finger, Sakura hurriedly lowered her hand, and her mouth stretched out in a grin. "I didn't cheat. I just worked super hard."

"Worked hard? How?"

"Memorizing."

On the other side of the door were stairs leading down to the basement. As they descended the brick stairs one by one, Sakura continued.

"Those cards were all super old, right? Some were dirty or bent, but each card was slightly different. So while I pretended to check the pictures, I memorized them all."

"All sixty cards?" Sasuke stared at her.

"Yeah." She nodded. "But in the beginning, I was a bit sketchy on a few of them, so I was really nervous in the first round. It's a trick I learned when I was training with my master."

Her voice softened.

"Even though she's honestly terrible at gambling, Lady Tsunade hated to lose. So, at first, I was careful and deliberately let her win. But then she'd get all excited and would keep me there playing with her for days. But she'd get bored after a series of draws. Her face would get all pale, and she'd say, 'Let's just stop already.'"

She was probably freaked out, not bored.

While Sasuke wondered whether or not he should say this out loud, they reached the bottom of the stairs.

The cobweb-covered stacks were stuffed artlessly with large and small scrolls, bound books, and documents in a variety of sizes. For all the supposed importance of these books, preserved and kept off-limits for viewing, they weren't actually all that well cared for.

Sakura touched a wall and sent her chakra crawling into it, to see if there were any traps set up in the basement space. By following the movement of her spreading chakra, she could get a rough idea of the layout of the entire building.

"Huh?" she said suddenly.

"What is it?" Sasuke asked.

"It looks like there's another room on the other side of that wall." She turned her gaze to the wall further back. In the direction of the main building.

She closed her eyes and concentrated harder on the flow of her chakra. It was because she had such excellent chakra control that she could use this technique to search the structure of a building using chakra inorganically.

"It's a spiral staircase," she said. "It connects with...the director's office on the fourth floor."

"There aren't any stairs leading down from the first floor in the main building." Sasuke frowned. "So this means there's a hidden underground room, and it's separated from the library basement by a single wall?"

A basement room that could only be reached via the director's office. Basically, a secret room.

"Suspicious. Seems like it'd be hiding something important."

"We'll check it out later. It'd be great if this hidden room was connected with the ultra particles." Sakura was curious about this mystery room, but finding *Map of the Heavens* took priority. She took her hand off the wall, wandered the low stacks, and searched for the shelf listed in the catalogue.

"I found it. Here. *Map of the Heavens*."

She pulled a book about as wide as her shoulders from the "I" shelf. The plain cover was a deep blue, like the slowly darkening evening sky. The fact that it was a bit rough to the touch likely meant that pigments made from crushed minerals had been used on it. The spine was decorated with the words *Map of the Heavens* in gold.

"It'd be great if this book gave us some kind of clue," she said. And as her hand flipped the cover open, she gasped.

Sasuke peered at the page from over her shoulder. "Sai?" He unexpectedly whispered the name of his village comrade, but this was a natural leap for his mind to make.

The page held an ink painting in black. Drawn in flowing brushstrokes was a tanuki parent and child frolicking on a dune.

Sakura brought the page to her nose and caught the scent of charred oil mixed in with the grassy smell of glue. She'd smelled this any number of times when she was assigned to missions with Sai. The painting had been done with ink made of soot and thinned with water, the very same painting style as that handed down in the Land of Fire.

But as far as she or Sasuke knew, this style of painting using ink did not exist in the Land of Redaku.

"Then the book was made outside of this country?" Sasuke frowned. "It's also possible that someone from abroad came here and painted it."

"An outsider who came to the Land of Redaku and stayed here a long, long time ago," Sakura mused.

The same person popped into both of their heads.

The Sage of Six Paths.

One hypothesis was that he had painted this picture while he was visiting this land. Ink drawing techniques reached other countries after that, including the Land of Fire, and were still in use right up to the present day. But they had gradually died out in the Land of Redaku. Accounting for the fact that this observatory had sat forgotten for many years, it was certainly a plausible hypothesis.

The very first page was an ink painting of tanuki playing on a dune. On the next page, a giant. On the page after that, a watchfire; after that, a cat; and then a monkey, cow, elderly person, and shepherd.

"They're the same as the Star Lines cards," Sasuke murmured, as he checked the last page.

Tanuki parent and child playing on the dune. Giant being born from the earth. Orange watchfire. Cat staring at a lantern flame. Monkey drawing on the ground with a tree branch. Cow peering into a pot. Elderly person with white hair and a cane. Shepherd looking up at the night sky through a glass bead. Turtle climbing a rocky mountain. White horse swimming in the ocean. Frog and slug crawling through the bog. Tree trunk with sap oozing down the side.

The images in the twelve ink drawings were indeed a perfect match for those on the Star Lines picture cards.

"I don't get it. How are these paintings connected with the location of the ultra particles?" Sakura traced the ink-stained pages, and then her hand stopped abruptly.

When she looked closely, she could see small dots scattered about on each of the paintings, as though drawn with the tip of a brush. And the images of the tanuki and turtle and others looked as though they had been drawn over these dots, to connect them with lines.

"These aren't ordinary ink paintings," she said in a flash of insight. "They're constellations."

"Constellations?" Sasuke parroted.

"Diagrams of plants or animals using the arrangement of stars in the sky. You know. We have them in the Land of Fire too—Taurus, Aries, all of those. You were born on July twenty-third, so you're a Leo," Sakura explained as she turned to the page with the drawing of the slug. Five small dots were arranged in a zigzag along the tips of the antenna on the slug's head. "Look, these five dots. It's the exact same arrangement as the Dipper."

The Dipper was the name for a line of five stars that could be seen from spring through summer. The distinctive meandering formation seemed to match up with the dots on this painting.

"I get it." Sasuke nodded. "The Dipper's in the sky from the end of spring into the summer. So then is this slug a constellation to express that period?"

"There are exactly twelve paintings, so maybe each one depicts the constellation that hangs in the moonlit sky in the months from January to December," Sakura said. "We might find a clue if we change the order of the constellations."

"Change the order?" He frowned. "That'll take some time."

The Land of Redaku was quite far from the Land of Fire. The way the stars looked in the night sky was undoubtedly quite different here than it was back home.

"Oh, it'll be fine," Sakura told him lightly and looked around at the documents piled up in the room. "There are plenty of astronomical records stored here. Give me a couple days, and I think I can figure out the order of the paintings by comparing them with past observations. Rearrange them by months."

"I can always count on you." Sasuke was sincere in his admiration of her abilities. He flipped through the *Map of the Heavens* on the viewing table.

He was sure that Sakura would be able to identify the time period for each painting and the order they should be in. But there was something about the lineup of animals selected that bothered him somehow.

Giant.

Tanuki.

Cat.

Monkey.

Cow.

Turtle.

White horse.

Frog and slug.

And the shepherd and old person. Tree trunk and watchfire.

He felt like he'd seen this arrangement before. Not on the Star Lines picture cards. Further back in time, somewhere. Like he'd seen an old person, cat, turtle, and monkey all together.

"Sasuke, what's wrong?" Sakura looked up at him.

"Oh…" He was about to close the book when he noticed something wedged into the spine. "Hm?"

It was a piece of straw paper folded in four with a short text scrawled on it in cursive style.

X Month X Day The stars increased.

An incomprehensible note.

But what caught both Sasuke's and Sakura's eyes was not the text, but the figure drawn below it.

It was an all too familiar hieroglyph. Any shinobi in the village of Konohagakure who'd been recognized as an adult wore this symbol on their person. And in the most conspicuous place on their entire body. At the academy, they'd learned that this glyph came from a shinobi placing a tree leaf on their head and training to focus their energy. The symbol of Konohagakure, combining a fallen leaf and a whirlpool.

"Why… What is the mark of Konoha doing here?"

The two of them looked at each other, at a loss for words.

They had discovered the glyph of their village in a faraway observatory, inside an astronomical text written in the distant past.

The words "the stars increased," the Konoha mark, and the observatory. Neither Sasuke nor Sakura were able to find anything to connect these three truly disparate elements.

The next morning.

Sakura pressed a scrap of paper into Sasuke's hand as she passed him in the hallway while he was on his way to the cafeteria.

When he went to a spot where no one was around and opened it, he saw the constellations from the previous day rearranged by month. It seemed that Sakura had identified the observation period for each one in a single night.

January: Tanuki parent and child playing on a dune.

February: Cat staring at a lantern flame.

March: Turtle climbing a rocky mountain.

April: Monkey drawing on the ground with a tree branch.

May: White horse swimming in the ocean.

June: Frog and slug crawling through the bog.

July: Tree trunk with sap oozing down the side.

August: Cow peering into a pot.

September: Orange watchfire.

October: Giant being born from the earth.

November: Shepherd looking up at the night sky through a glass bead.

December: Elderly person with white hair and a cane.

The animals were concentrated from January to August. September was the watchfire—flames. October, the giant. And November and December were people. Shepherd and old person.

On the back of the note was a quick, scribbled message.

Tomorrow, 2:00 pm. Library.

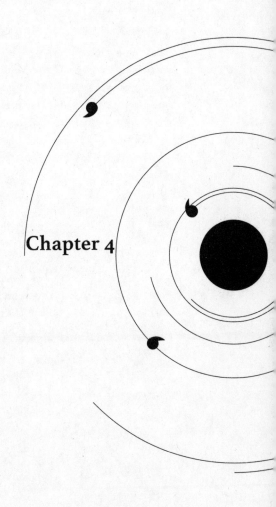

Chapter 4

Once again, as they did every day, the prisoners headed for the worksite, thoroughly exhausted.

Roused from their beds at the crack of dawn, they ate whatever food that was set out for them before leaving for work. And by the time the sun was beginning to set, they had supper and a bath before returning to their cells. From the outside, it looked like a life with zero freedom, but each prisoner filled the gaps in their rigidly defined days with their own tiny personal pleasures, something that freed them from the control of authority, if only for a moment.

For Penzila, it was gambling. For Ganno, it was painting his toenails. And for Jiji, that something was guessing when Meno was on duty.

"Oh, I did it! I got it again today!" Jiji cried out excitedly when he heard the creaking of the boards in the hallway. "That's ten days in a row!"

"Your hunches are the real deal," Ganno said, his back rounded as always, his entire being focused on his toenails. "It's been three days since Meno showed up in the evening."

Guessing when Meno would patrol the prisoner residence in the evening was a pastime that did neither harm nor good, much like guessing whether a man or a woman would walk down the street next. But Jiji's predictions were curiously accurate, and both Ganno and Penzila kept track of how long his current winning streak continued. Unlike with the guards, where the same faces appeared at the same time every day, Meno's patrols were at the lizard's whim.

"You just never know with animals. My girlfriend's into horseback riding, so she's taught me all kinds of stuff."

At Meno's approach, Penzila hurriedly moved to a corner of the cell. A lover of gambling and yet cowardly, he hated to catch sight of Meno.

"I can't believe you made a game out of Meno, Jiji," he said. "You're not scared?"

"Stupid." Jiji snorted. "It's fine. So long as no rules are broken, Meno won't attack."

A large shadow stepped into the light of the paper lantern in the cell. Soon, Meno came into view, marching forward with large heavy steps, very much the sentry.

"See, look," Jiji said, and picked up a branch Ganno used for a paintbrush. He pushed it through the bars and waved the leafy tip at Meno.

The lizard's gaze turned toward the branch, its yellow eyes bobbing in time with the movement.

"C'mere," Jiji said amiably.

Meno slowly came over to the bars. It snorted and grazed the dancing leaves with its nose, almost like a cat playing with a toy.

"It really came," Penzila murmured, stunned. "Huh? How come?"

"This guy's always curled up under the almond tree, right? But it's not like he eats the nuts or anything. I'm pretty sure he just likes the smell. You could probably touch him."

Jiji looked back at Penzila, and the other man leaped back.

"What? Me?!" Penzila firmly shook his head. "No, no, no, no! Absolutely not! I like my arm right where it is, thank you."

"Okay, Sasuke then," Jiji said.

"I actually need my arm too," Sasuke told him.

"You guys are no fun." Jiji sighed and looked at Ganno.

Dubiously, Ganno set his brush down and stood up. "You really think it's okay?"

He slowly pushed a skinny, tanned arm through the bars and reached out to Meno's flat forehead with bony fingers. He stroked the skin, which was hard like scales, a few times, and Meno's narrow eyes opened the slightest bit.

"Whoa," Penzila breathed in astonishment, eyes wide as saucers. "Holy smokes."

"Sasuke, you wanna try?" Ganno asked.

"No, I'll pass." Sasuke shook his head. If Meno remembered that he had sliced into his belly, he might just bite him to get revenge.

"Maybe I'll give it a go." Penzila slowly stood up, apparently emboldened by Ganno's success.

"Here." Ganno ceded his place to his cellmate.

Penzila stepped forward timidly and grabbed onto the bars. The tips of his toes projected ever so slightly over the boundary between room and hall.

Instantly, Meno's eyes snapped wide open.

"Get back!" Faster than Sasuke could move, Jiji grabbed Penzila's shoulder and yanked him back.

At the same time, the charging Meno slammed into the door. His talons came through the bars and knocked over the lantern.

"Gaaunh!"

Hot oil from the lantern splashed onto his stomach, and Meno let out a cry as he leaped back. Then he ran down the hallway, as if fleeing.

The lantern oil dish had broken and the pieces scattered, but fortunately, the flames didn't set fire to anything else and simply snuffed out on the cold floor.

"Whoa." Knocked backward onto his bottom, Penzila sat up, his face pale. "That scared me."

"I was the one who was scared, you dodo." Jiji whapped him on the head, and Penzila started trembling after the fact, perhaps recoiling from the experience.

"Why'd he come charging all of a sudden like that?" he asked. "He was being so nice a second before."

"Your feet," Sasuke replied, picking up the pieces of the oil tray. "They were sticking out of the cell."

During their free time before lights out, they were allowed to do whatever they wanted as long as they remained in their cells. But the moment they set even one foot outside their barred doors, they were in violation of the rules.

"Huh? Just for that?" Penzila furrowed his brow. "We can put our hands out, but not our feet?"

"We're not allowed to leave our cells," Jiji said. "I guess for Meno, the line for 'leave' is whether or not our feet are on the floor."

Penzila nodded in understanding. "Thanks, Jiji. Sorry. If it hadn't been for you, I would've got my face eaten off by Meno."

"Say sorry to Meno, not me," Jiji told him. "He let out a mighty howl when that oil hit him."

"Apologize to me too. Honestly, wasting our precious oil." Ganno looked annoyed as he crawled along the floor, soaking up the spilled oil with a piece of paper.

Sasuke poured fresh oil into the dish and lit it with Chidori Fireworks when no one was looking since he couldn't be bothered to use a flint.

The oil-soaked wick flickered a bright orange, reminding Sasuke of the Hokage. He wondered how Naruto was doing in the village. And then he wondered about Kurama.

"You guys do something?" a guard called, attracted by the noise. "There was a real racket there."

Jiji and Penzila already had their cover stories straight: they had just been fighting a little.

Meanwhile, Sasuke's eyes were drawn to the lantern's flame.

One of the twelve constellations took the watchfire as a motif. The *Map of the Heavens* was all black ink, but on the Star Lines picture cards, the fire was a vivid orange, the exact same color as Kurama's fur. The shape of the burning flames was almost like nine tails fanned out.

Almost like?

Sasuke blinked and stared at the lantern. A small orange light, generating heat, maintaining life, and lapping up oxygen. The flame before him was quite unlike the watchfire depicted on the picture card. Only the color was the same. The orange of combustion, of the oxygen reaction.

All that was orange in this world was not flames, however. Was the September constellation on the picture card really a watchfire?

What if it was not actually flames, but nine fox tails?

•

The library, 1400 hours.

"It's a biju," Sasuke announced immediately, after slipping out of work to meet Sakura at a shelf on the west side of the library.

"What?" Sakura uttered.

No preamble, no "hello how are you," just cutting straight to the chase. Sakura was used to Sasuke's bluntness, but even she needed a moment to process and react.

"I'm talking about the constellations in *Map of the Heavens*," he said. "Ten of the twelve constellations depict tailed beasts."

"Oh!" Sakura, catching on.

The tanuki parent and child playing on the dune was One Tail, Shukaku, the tailed beast that had the appearance of a supernatural tanuki.

The cat staring at the lantern flame was Two Tails, Matatabi.

The turtle climbing a rocky mountain was Three Tails, Isobu.

The monkey drawing on the ground with a tree branch was Four Tails, Son Goku.

The white horse swimming in the ocean was Five Tails, Kokuo.

The frog and slug crawling through the bog were Six Tails, Saiken.

The seventh constellation was the tree trunk.

"Seven Tails—Chomei was a rhinoceros beetle, right?" Sasuke opened *Map of the Heavens* on the viewing table and turned to the constellation in question.

Looking closely at the image, he noticed a large hollow near the center of the trunk and rhinoceros beetles swarming to the sap dripping down from it.

"Mmm. This constellation isn't the tree itself. It's depicting the rhinoceros beetles on it."

The cow peering into a pot was Eight Tails, Gyuki. The pot was likely an octopus pot.

What had looked like a watchfire was the fox with nine tails. The figure of Nine Tails, Kurama, from behind.

And the constellation for October, the giant being born from the earth, was Ten Tails.

"Then the last two are..."

The elderly person with white hair and a cane, and the shepherd looking up at the night sky.

"The Sage of Six Paths and the astronomer Tatar?" Sakura suggested.

"Probably." He nodded.

The Sage of Six Paths was said to have been on the brink of death when he split the chakra of Ten Tails into nine parts, after *Map of the Heavens* was drawn. It wasn't clear if the nine tailed beasts had any connection with the animals in these constellations or not.

Either way, the Sage of Six Paths had gone out of his way to make sure there would be twelve of these constellations, adding himself and Tatar to the ten beasts. Had they used the same calendar back then as they did now? Had he matched the number of constellations to the number of months, or was there some particular meaning in the number twelve?

"Sakura," he said. "What did you call me to the library for?"

"Oh, right." She lifted her face from *Map of the Heavens.* "We've got an excuse to sneak into Zansul's rooms. I heard a messenger's coming today from the capital."

"The capital?" Sasuke repeated. "From the prime minister?"

"Mm hmm." She nodded.

He knew about the prime minister of the Land of Redaku based on the information Kakashi had sent. He was conspiring with Queen Marina to start a war with another country. Why on earth would this prime minister be sending a messenger to the director?

"This is our chance," Sakura told him. "We pretend to be the messenger and meet with Zansul ourselves."

•

Arriving at the front gate of the observatory at long last, Fandal removed his filthy cloak.

The tall wall before him blocked his view of the premises. The majestic front gate was protected by several layers of iron bars. The brick building beyond it was grey and dull and bathed in the muted sunlight. It was already the season when dandelions began to bloom near the capital, but he couldn't see even the earliest signs of spring in this area.

Just breathing the air made him depressed.

Reassuring himself that he would leave as soon as he'd delivered the message entrusted to him by the prime minister, Fandal asked to be shown inside.

"Welcome."

He had assumed that he would be welcomed by some stern-faced guard, but it was a young woman who appeared before him. Perhaps because of her coloring—cherry pink hair and jade eyes—he felt like the dull, stagnant air suddenly grew lighter and brighter.

"Oh," he said. "I've come from the capital of the Land of Redaku with a message from the prime minister for Director Zansul. I am Fandal, a government official."

He showed the woman the staff with the ridiculously large hawk statue on the end that was proof of his status as an official messenger.

"We heard you were coming." The woman smiled. "I know you must be tired after your long journey, but would you be able to meet with him right away? The director is naturally quite busy, but he just happens to be free at the moment."

"Of course." Fandal nodded and followed the woman into the main building.

"What is this business from the prime minister then?" she asked him in a natural tone that suggested casual conversation.

Fandal cocked his head to one side. "A good question. I don't know the details myself. I was simply told by the prime minister to come and inquire about the progress."

"Progress?" the woman replied. "Progress with what?"

"I have no idea. I was just told he would understand."

An ambassador necessarily did not ask questions about the luggage or letters he carried.

"Is this your first time meeting Director Zansul?" The woman considerately asked him another question to prevent any uncomfortable silences.

"Formally, yes," Fandal said. "But I've seen him any number of times when he's come to the palace."

"You have? When was the last time the director visited the capital again?"

"It was last summer. He came to visit the prime minister. My wife works as a maid at the palace, and she was put in charge of Lord Zansul's care, as a matter of fact."

They continued to chat about trivialities as they walked down the long hallway.

He was shown to a large room on the third floor, and as soon as he stepped inside, the scent of dust assaulted his nostrils. The room was filled with instruments likely used in astronomical observations. A clock-like disc with several gears, a model of the heavens with mysterious planets surrounding a red star. Considering that this was an observatory, the existence of such a room was only natural, but it very much did not look like a space in which to receive visitors.

"Err, where is Lord Zansul?" Fandal grew uneasy and turned back to the woman who had brought him here.

"He'll be here shortly." She smiled.

Thmp. Someone hit the back of his neck, and Fandal slipped out of consciousness as though he'd fallen asleep.

"There we go." Sakura turned herself into the spitting image of Fandal with transformation jutsu, put a hand on her hip, and turned toward Sasuke. "Okay, your turn."

"I'm transforming too?" he asked.

"That way's safer."

The strategy was simple.

Sakura would be the prime minister's envoy, meet with Zansul, and buy time while she tried to get information on *Map of the Heavens* and the prime minister's plans. During that time, Sasuke would sneak into the basement and find exactly what was going on down there. They would each handle any problems that came up on their own. Later, they would use genjutsu on Fandal and make him believe he had met with Zansul before sending him back to the capital.

"I guess it's got to be this if you're going to transform." Sakura held out Fandal's staff. Since changing size cost chakra, the best plan was for Sasuke to turn into something as close to his actual height as possible.

"This?" He looked skeptical.

It was more difficult to transform into an inorganic object than a person. He'd turned himself into a shuriken and a kunai before, but a staff was a first.

He'd give it a try.

After touching it several times to check the material, Sasuke worked his chakra.

Pop!

He turned into an exact copy of the staff and clattered to the floor.

"Perfect," Sakura said as she picked him up.

He felt sort of strange, but with this their preparations were complete. Now to go and face the director.

Tapping the staff/Sasuke on the floor, Sakura mimicked Fandal's mannerisms and movements as she climbed the stairs. She knocked on the heavy door of the director's office and announced herself.

Zansul poked his head out the door and invited Sakura inside without the slightest hesitation.

For Sasuke, who so often worked alone on missions outside the village, it was a novel thing to work a mission with a comrade.

He couldn't imagine getting this close to a difficult enemy so easily on his own.

Zansul urged Sakura to take a seat on the sofa and sat down in an armchair opposite it. Further back, there was a desk with a modern design that seemed very un-Redaku-like.

This was Zansul's study.

As far as she could tell from investigating it in advance with her chakra, there was a bedroom further back, separated by a transom with no door, and somewhere in that bedroom, there was a door to the staircase that led to the basement.

"And how is the prime minister?" Zansul asked placidly as he leaned back in a leisurely manner. "It's been over six months since we last met."

"He's quite well," Sakura replied. "As is Queen Marina."

"Wonderful. I suppose she's accustomed to her official duties by now."

Once they had exchanged their lighthearted greetings, Sakura casually turned her gaze toward the window.

"Oh dear. It seems as though it rained, hm?"

"What?" Zansul stood up and looked outside.

The moment his gaze was elsewhere, Sakura tossed the cane forward along the floor. It slid soundlessly across the shaggy rug and stopped just before the boundary between study and bedroom.

"It isn't raining. Perhaps you missaw?" Zansul said, lowering himself into his chair, back turned to the cane.

Sasuke released the transformation jutsu without any sound or vibration to return to his original form. Making sure his aura was undetectable, he stepped into the bedroom, found a blind spot against the wall, and took a look around the room.

Wooden bed, bookcase. A metal door built into the far wall. It probably opened onto the staircase to the basement, but unfortunately, if he stood in front of it, he would be in full view of the study.

He glanced back to see how things were going with Sakura.

"I'd heard that the water shortage in the capital is serious," Zansul remarked.

"It does appear so, yes. Although the palace is given priority, with food and drink coming there first, so it hasn't felt dire," Sakura replied.

Zansul was talking with Sakura, his back to Sasuke. Maybe he had a chance here.

Sasuke stepped out in front of the door, boldly revealing himself. He prayed that Zansul had carelessly forgotten to lock it and pulled on the handle, but sadly, the door remained firmly shut.

Could he force it open?

Plenty of shinobi used ninjutsu to pick locks, but the method differed from person to person. Kakashi often used the heat of Fire Style to melt the metal part. Shikamaru inserted a long, thin shadow into the keyhole to turn the cylinders. Naruto would make it move with a very small-scale bit of turbulence.

Given that he excelled in Fire Style, Sasuke often followed Kakashi's example and melted the lock itself, but he didn't want to leave any trace of himself here, so he decided to use a different method.

He looked back and signaled to Sakura to buy a little more time. Catching this, Sakura leaned forward.

"The truth is, I've actually seen you before, Lord Zansul. You visited the palace last summer, did you not? I was pleased to be able to say hello to you."

"Is that so?" Zansul replied. "Last summer, that would not have been long after the former king passed, hm? Queen Marina is still young, so I suppose the prime minister is terribly busy. And speaking of, would you mind telling me on what matter he sent you here?"

"Of course, yes. But before that, one thing. The maid who looked after you while you stayed at the palace was in fact my own wife. Perhaps you remember her? Let me remind you..."

While Sakura bought time with chitchat, Sasuke touched a finger to the keyhole and kneaded his chakra. He formed Earth Style sand in the exact same shape as the hole and improvised a master key. He couldn't make something as complicated as the library key, but fortunately, the lock before him was a type that he had copied in the past.

But it wouldn't work the way he had made the ring for Sakura. Fine chakra control was required to harden the crumbling earth, match it with the inside of the lock, and create a key.

"...And so, you see, for my wife, it ended up being such a wonderful experience to serve you, Lord Zansul. She is so deeply grateful to you." Sakura was doing her best to stall.

"Please tell her that I appreciated her good care. Now then, it is about time that I heard this message from the prime minister." Zansul was growing impatient.

"Yes, I suppose you're right. Please excuse me for going on at length like this. The prime minister often scolds me for being too talkative when I am meant to be a messenger. I believe it's likely because I was raised in a household with six older sisters. My mother and my grandmother also both loved to talk—"

"Fandal." Zansul's voice grew harder. "I would hear your message."

"Oh, yes, of course." Fandal/Sakura shrugged gracefully. "It is a strange one, but the message this time is a single question. 'How is progress?' I personally have no idea what it means."

"Heh! How like the prime minister. Progress is good. Please tell him that if it's to Nagare, we will be able to send firepower within a few hours, a few days if it's to the capital, at any time we receive that request."

"I understand. Incidentally, this 'firepower'—exactly how much?" Sakura attempted to pry more.

"You are merely a messenger, yes? It wouldn't do to tell you specific numbers. Have no worries. The prime minister will understand." Zansul remained cryptic.

While Sakura stalled to give Sasuke more time, Sasuke somehow managed to finish creating the key. Or he should have, but when he turned it in the lock, it broke off at the base. Was it not strong enough? Restraining the urge to click his tongue, he touched the broken cross-section with a finger and worked his chakra once more.

Uncharacteristically, he was slightly flustered. If he had been on this mission alone, he would have been fine with some danger, but Sakura was with him now.

"I overstepped by asking such a question, didn't I? I do sincerely apologize."

"No, no. Anyway, Fandal, what happened to your staff?"

"My staff?"

"You had one when you came into the room, didn't you? I don't seem to see it anywhere now."

The chakra-formed earth hardened in his hand. Certain that it was properly attached to the cross-section of the broken key, Sasuke turned the key once again.

This time, it didn't break.

However.

Chak! The spring lifting echoed in the small space.

"Hm?" Zansul started to look behind him and then brought his gaze back to the front, surprised by the *thmp!* he heard a heartbeat later.

Sakura tapped the floor forcefully with the real staff, which she had pulled out of her cloak.

"My staff is right here."

In the moment that Sakura drew Zansul's attention, Sasuke opened the door and slipped inside.

It was pitch black. Dusty, humid, and smelling of mold. When he called up a Fire Style fire and looked around, he saw stairs descending in a spiral at his feet.

This was the entrance to the basement.

He didn't have much time. He killed the sound of his steps and started down the stairs.

Just when it seemed he'd gone five flights or so, an iron door rose up to block his way. He created a key with Earth Style as he had before and unlocked it.

When he gently pushed the heavy door open, cool air poured out over him, followed by the sound of wings flapping.

Birds?

"Buk-gawk!"

Chickens.

Buk, buk.

They came over, waggling their tail feathers, and surrounded Sasuke in the blink of an eye, pecking at his shoes and legs. There were maybe forty—no, fifty of them.

Why would there be chickens down here?

Unlike in the stuffy spiral staircase, there were ventilation openings in the basement, ensuring a bare minimum of airflow. The vegetable scraps in the feed boxes scattered about were much fresher than what the prisoners were given to eat. There was also plenty of clean water, and it was clear that the birds were well cared for by humans.

Cut pieces of rock were stacked against the wall. They were irregularly shaped, like warped statues, with dirt from the area stuck to their surfaces. He had seen prisoners ordered to carry similar rocks when he was working outside.

In the basement, with feathers scattered all about, Sasuke stood rooted to the spot, perplexed.

A large number of chickens and a pile of rocks.

What exactly was this place?

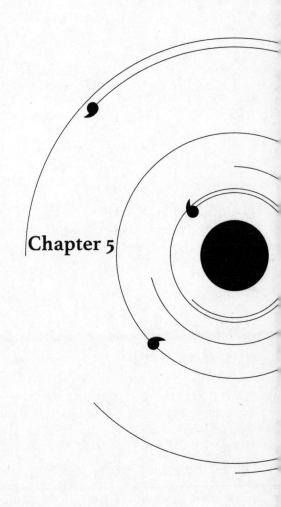

Chapter 5

Four days after the prime minister's messenger Fandal's visit to Zansul, Sakura received a message from Kakashi via hawk.

The prime minister of the Land of Redaku had joined with Queen Marina and invaded the village of Nagare. In the face of this, the queen's younger brother prince Nanara had decided to stage a coup d'état and seize power. Kakashi was planning to help the prince.

Fandal had come to ask Zansul about "progress." And Zansul had replied that they would be able to send firepower right away. From this new message, she had to assume that Zansul's firepower was to support the prime minister's troops.

But where exactly was he hiding all this force in this observatory, so far away in the north?

She summed up what she knew of the current situation in a reply to Kakashi and affixed the paper to the leg of a hawk that wore a red piece of fabric tied around it. The hawk squawked unhappily, insisting on at least a single night's rest, so she let it peck at a scrap of dried meat as a reward to soothe its displeasure and appease it before sending it back to Kakashi. Then Sakura headed for the cafeteria.

It was just suppertime. The line of prisoners with trays stretched out into the hallway.

She wanted to tell Sasuke what Kakashi had said, but she couldn't see him in the hallway or in the cafeteria itself. Ignoring the stares of the ruder prisoners, she sat at a table near the window and propped her chin up in her hands.

None of this made any sense.

The relationship between Zansul and the prime minister. The firepower Zansul mentioned. The location of the ultra particles. The meaning behind *Map of the Heavens* and its ink paintings of the twelve constellations. The chickens and the pile of rocks against the wall that Sasuke had discovered in the basement.

She couldn't piece all the fragments together to see a whole picture. Maybe the basement didn't even matter. Maybe Zansul just kept chickens and collected stone sculpture as a hobby. But then again, no. That couldn't have been it.

"I don't get it," she moaned and threw herself back in her chair.

"You mind if I sit here, Doc?" asked an older man from the other side of the table.

She shook her head. "No, go ahead."

It was Ganno, Sasuke's cellmate, the strange man whose hobby was painting pictures on his toenails.

After moistening his throat with the watered-down tea from the blackened samovar, Ganno turned his eyes to the view outside. "Sun's already setting, hm?"

"Mm hmm," Sakura agreed and stared at the rays of the sun falling on the table. The red light poured in from low in the sky and was so sharp and clear she could almost hold it in her hand.

"For a long time, I thought that sunset meant that the sun was going down," Ganno said lazily, still looking out the window. "But that's not actually it, I guess. The ground we're riding on here

goes and spins on its own and moves away from the sun.
I always figured it was the sky that was moving."

"I was surprised when I learned that too," she said. "We're
so quick to think that people are the center of things, hm?"

He smiled gently and turned his eyes on her hand. "You're
wearing a ring today, Doc. Are you married?"

"I am." She nodded. "But the ring gets in the way when I'm
working, so I often take it off."

"Working up in a place like this, I guess you don't get home
too often."

"Well..." The truth was, if she wasn't working way out here,
she'd almost never get to see her husband.

"What kind of man's your husband?" Ganno continued.

"He's very kind." She'd wanted to reply with something in-
nocuous and honest, but she found herself wanting to say more
and added, "And he's very pure."

Knowing that Ganno didn't know who her husband was,
it was easy to let herself keep talking fondly.

"Sometimes, he's too blunt, and it makes things tough for
him and everyone who knows him. His thinking can jump from
one extreme to the other. But I like that about him. And he's
very attractive physically, but he has absolutely zero interest
in that. I love that about him. Although it does worry me sometimes."

"Oh yeah? That Sasuke's a lucky guy."

Thud.

The hands propping up her chin slid away, and Sakura's
face hit the table. Ganno chuckled.

"What? H-h-how do you," she stammered. "Oh, I mean, my
husband's not, I mean..."

"It's him, hm?" Ganno nodded, convinced. "He used to sit
here and stare out the window all the time. But he hasn't been
doing that lately. Not since you came. I always wondered what it

was he was looking at, but now, I finally get it. He was wondering when that tree was going to bloom."

"B-bloom?" Sakura said. "No, um, that's, anyway, why would you think Sasuke's my husband..."

"Your hair's such a pretty color. You gotta take care of it." Ganno beamed like a father giving a child a pinwheel and left without further explanation.

Alone again at the table, Sakura and her head were full of question marks.

What does my hair have to do with anything...

Confused, she turned her gaze out the window and sought out the tree that Ganno had mentioned.

There was just one tree with flowers. On clipped branches a single layer of small flowers bloomed. The light pink petals were so tiny, they threatened to disappear from sight if she blinked.

She stared at them for a while, and when she finally realized what Ganno meant, she turned red up to her ears.

Sasuke had been waiting for the sakura to bloom.

The tree wasn't actually a sakura cherry tree, but a type of almond that bloomed at high altitudes. Which only made sense. Sakura wouldn't bloom in a place with a climate like this.

After returning to the infirmary, Sakura caught a glimpse of her face in the metal tongue depressor and discovered that she was beaming. Maybe Ganno had simply gotten the wrong idea, but it made her incredibly happy to think that Sasuke had been thinking about her while waiting for the pink flowers to bloom.

Sakura had also kept a flower on her desk at work for the same reason.

She had picked up the camellia, now with its stem artlessly tucked into a glass bottle, where it had fallen from the hedge in the courtyard. Camellias always reminded her of Sasuke. It was a flower with only two options: bloom at the tip of the stem or drop off to the ground. She thought the flower's determined instinct was exactly like Sasuke's.

The bottle with the camellia shone a lovely orange, wrapped in the light of the setting sun. Soon, the sun would sink completely.

No. I guess it's actually us that sets, like Ganno said.

Even though she knew this fact, she still felt in her heart that it was the sun doing the setting. *I've got no right to be a doctor, thinking like this,* she thought with a wry smile. For scientists—and that group included doctors—it was essential to eschew subjectivity and look at things objectively. And yet here she was.

In that sense, it hadn't been particularly scientific of Tatar to connect the arrangements of the stars with tanuki and monkeys in *Map of the Heavens*. The stars may have looked like a tanuki or a turtle when viewed from the ground, but there was no astronomical meaning in that.

Still...

Sakura felt like she could understand a little at least how the astronomer must have felt, connecting star with star and associating the outlines with the shapes of animals. It had to have been the same mindset that led her to talk to the cells she cultivated in petri dishes. Working with them on a daily basis, she felt a fondness for them that led to a sort of playfulness in her. Even if the object of study was something inorganic, a human being was providing observation and subjectivity to the inorganic subject.

The signs that shinobi wove were no doubt named after the constellations for the same reason.

In front of her chest, Sakura brought her hands together in the sign for rat. The shape her hands made had absolutely no connection with the actual animal. But the sign needed a name of some kind, so the shinobi of the long-distant past had given this combination the title "rat" for the sake of convenience. Since there were twelve basic hand combinations used in weaving signs, the twelve animals of the zodiac fit perfectly.

Sakura abruptly lifted her gaze.

Twelve zodiac signs... Twelve?

"Ah!"

Sakura stood up forcefully enough to knock her chair over and dashed out of the infirmary.

The lower part of the evening sky was already violet, bits of cloud scattered here and there.

Sasuke was sitting on the brick roof doing his job for the day: collecting apricots.

"When they get their sights set on you the guards always end up nabbing me too. Aah, I'm so tired," Jiji sighed as he artlessly reached out for a branch from the pile in front of him. He neatly twisted the stem of the mature small fruit and carefully pulled it free so as not to damage it, and then held up the freed fruit so Sasuke could polish its dusty skin with one hand.

He and Jiji were on the roof of the main building, in the middle of a job the guards had ordered them to stay and do after regular working hours were over. It was only natural that Sasuke had been nominated for the overtime, given that he was a target for the guards' harassment, and having often been paired with Sasuke in the past, Jiji had been chosen as a bonus fruit harvester.

"They brought this tree up from the capital, huh?" Jiji remarked. "Apricots don't grow well way out here."

"I guess." Sasuke nodded. "They must bring new ones from the palace every so often."

"We've never gotten apricots in our meals. S'pose only the director and the guards get to eat them. Dammit."

"Eat one now," Sasuke said. He picked out a nicely shaped fruit from the mountain of apricots he'd polished and tossed it into his mouth.

"Listen you, quit that," Jiji said. "You'll catch a beating if the guards find out."

Sasuke let Jiji's warning go in one ear and out the other as he crushed the fruit with his teeth. Maybe because of the climate, it was quite tart, which suited Sasuke's palate nicely as he didn't much care for sweets.

Jiji stood up, spread out his arms, and stretched to give his stiff shoulders some relief. "Aaaah."

Eyes drawn upward by his partner's movement, Sasuke looked out over the scene below.

They were deep in the mountains, and he could see the ridgelines of bare rock crossing back and forth in a kind of arabesque, like a diorama made only with sand. Devoid of color, the view continued like this as far as the eye could see. Or so he thought. But then he noticed on the ground at the base of the cliff on which the observatory stood an orange magatama bead.

No. A magatama wouldn't reflect the sky so neatly.

"Is there a lake near here?" he asked, and Jiji followed his gaze out to the magatama.

"Oh, the lake. It's pretty small, so loads of fellows don't even know it's there. Super clear, but no fish in it, meaning no one has any reason to go all the way down there. I heard it's a crater filled with rainwater. Meteor hit that spot way back in the old days."

A meteor.

Sasuke stepped toward the edge of the roof and peered at the lake below.

"..."

Outlined by pear-like curves, the lake water highlighted the sunset glow and sat there, still against the landscape, reflecting the tufts of clouds like a mirror. It was almost as if someone had scooped up the evening sky with a spoon and poured it into a hollow in the earth.

Sky?

"At this time of day, it gets a little reddish. But take a look at it during the day, and it's a perfect blue, very pretty. It's so clear you almost can't tell which one's the sky and which one's the lake," Jiji said, nearly in reverie.

"Jiji." Sasuke pushed the apricot branch in his hand at his work partner. "My stomach hurts. I'm leaving. You take care of the rest."

"Huh?" Jiji gaped at him.

"I'll take your next shift in the kitchen." He had no sooner spoken the words than he was turning on his heel and marching away.

"Hey! Where are you going?!"

He ignored Jiji's protests. He had to tell Sakura right away that he had solved one of the mysteries of *Map of the Heavens*.

"Ah!"

Sasuke ran into Sakura when he rounded the corner on the staircase landing.

They had both quenched their auras, so they very nearly slammed into each other. But the two shinobi were gifted with such impeccable reflexes that they each took a step back before the collision could happen.

"Sasuke, perfect timing," Sakura said excitedly and took his arm. "I figured out the mystery of *Map of the Heavens*."

"What?" He stared at her, and she dragged him into an empty room.

Once the door was closed behind them, Sakura said quietly, "Do you remember? That bit about how the Sage of Six Paths split the ultra particles into two and hid one half in the star that never strays and the other in the sky that fell to the earth?"

Sasuke nodded. It was in the text that Kakashi had sent them. Half of the ultra particles were hidden in the sky that fell to the earth and the other half in the star that never strays. To discover these locations, "revel" with the *Map of the Heavens*.

"The Sage of Six Paths is the originator of chakra. We should assume he used ninjutsu to hide the ultra particles, and you need signs to release ninjutsu. That means that hidden in the *Map of the Heavens* are the signs to get at the ultra particles."

Sakura pulled a scrap of paper out of her pocket and set it on top of the desk. It was covered in her handwriting.

"First, take a look at this. I numbered the zodiac signs and the constellations rearranged in chronological order."

1 Rat/Tanuki

2 Ox/Cat

3 Tiger/Turtle

4 Rabbit/Monkey

5 Dragon/White horse

6 Snake/Frog and slug

7 Horse/Tree trunk

8 Goat/Cow

9 Monkey/Watchfire

10 Rooster/Giant

11 Dog/Shepherd

12 Pig/Elderly person

"I see. Twelve zodiac signs and twelve constellations." Sasuke nodded in understanding as he ran his eyes over the words on the page. So the shepherd and the old person had been added to the ten animals to bulk up the number of constellations to twelve, in order to match the number of the signs of the zodiac. "But this alone doesn't tell us what the specific signs are."

"There's one more hint," she told him. "Star Lines."

"Star Lines?" Sasuke was still trying to catch on.

"'Reveling with the *Map of the Heavens*.' Don't you think that's a strange way of putting it? *Map of the Heavens* has nothing but ink paintings in it, so I mean, play with what? My guess is that the Star Lines picture cards originally went with the *Map of the Heavens*. I mean, the box the cards are in is way too big. It has too much extra space to be just for those little cards."

Indeed, the box was fairly large. Large enough for the oversized *Map of the Heavens* to fit inside nicely.

"The strongest hand in Star Lines is Star, the second strongest is Earth," she continued. "I think that Star is likely describing the star that never strays, and Earth the sky that fell to the earth."

"Makes sense." Sasuke turned his mind back to the match he'd watched between Sakura and Penzila. "The Star hand is made of the cards white horse, shepherd, cat, watchfire, giant, and turtle. So if we weave the signs of the constellations corresponding to those cards, we'll be able to find the ultra particles?"

White horse, shepherd, cat, watchfire, giant, and turtle—the signs contained in the six picture cards that made up the Star hand would then be dragon, dog, ox, monkey, rooster, and tiger, according to Sakura's notes. For Earth, it was ox, monkey, rat, snake, tiger, and pig. These were the signs they needed to obtain the ultra particles.

"That solves the mystery of the constellations. It's clear *what* we should do." Sakura ran her finger over the page of notes with a serious look on her face. "But I don't know *where* we should do it. What exactly are the sky that fell to the earth and the star that never strays pointing to?"

"I've got a guess as to the sky part."

"Right, I guess we... What?" Sakura jerked her head up.

Sasuke had dropped this bombshell bit of info so casually that Sakura only belatedly understood what he'd actually said.

"You've got a guess?" Sakura asked, stunned.

Her eyes were wide with surprise, and he looked back at her, his own face expressionless.

"I'll come get you tonight after lights out," he said and quickly left the room.

The sky was clear that night, so the stars were bright and visible.

Sasuke rapped on the window of the infirmary at the promised time.

"Come on," he said and jumped down from the second floor to the ground. He turned and looked up at her impatiently.

Not knowing what he was up to, Sakura took a second to remove her white lab coat and then jumped out of the window after him.

Killing their auras, they went over the wall and started down the cliff behind the observatory. After a few minutes of descending the rocky face, their field of view opened up. A small lake in a crater appeared up ahead of them.

Sakura stopped and gasped. "Wow!"

The calm surface of the water reflected the night sky perfectly. The particles of light dotting the black mirror was so beautiful that Sakura stood rooted to the spot and forgot to breathe.

"I guess it's called Sage Lake, after the Sage of Six Paths. The sky that fell to the earth... If that literally means a starry sky on earth, then there likely isn't a place that hits the mark better than this one," Sasuke explained.

Sakura barely even heard him.

The flat blue lake water embraced the entire night sky, and the moon with its rabbit-shaped shadow dropped an anchor in the bottom of the lake, shimmering at the edge of the shore. Everything present there was quiet and calm, making the actual reality feel mysterious and ethereal.

To think that a place like this was right behind the observatory.

She'd had few chances to leave the infirmary, so not only had she not known there was such a lake out here, she hadn't even realized that the sky above her was filled with such lovely stars every night.

"It's beautiful." Her eyes shone like a child's.

Sasuke watched her with a slight smile. "I wish we could show it to Sarada."

"Mm hmm." Sakura nodded. "She's been interested in astronomy lately. She went to the science fair at the research institute with Ino and them the other day. She's obsessed with reading about the moon and the stars."

She is?

Sasuke touched his wife's hand. Exposed to the outside air, her fingers had gotten cold, and he felt like they were more slender than he remembered. He was certain there were plenty of moments that he missed by not being with her.

Even without a ring, even if they couldn't always be together, the fact that Sakura was his wife and his family was never going to change. He was able to think like this thanks to a lesson from a good friend a long time ago. The most important thing was the bond they shared. He had a connection with Sakura that not even distance could touch. Even if he couldn't see her every day, she was his precious partner.

However.

Although he honestly believed this, he would abruptly be hit with a wave of sadness from time to time. Especially when he was on a lengthy mission and couldn't return to the village for long periods.

Not being able to hear each other's voice when they wanted to, not being together when they wanted to touch each other. Maybe it would be easier for them if they had something physical to hold on to, if they could see the bond they shared in an object like a ring.

"Sakura," he started. "Do you want a ring? Not one made with chakra. When we get back to the village. A regular one."

Correctly understanding Sasuke's intention despite the clumsiness of his question, Sakura thought for a moment. "Hmm. I *have* wanted one at times. But a ring probably doesn't suit my hands."

She smiled slightly and held her hands out in the moonlight.

Her hands, dry from constant washing, were the proof that Sakura had helped so many patients. At the same time, they were also Sasuke's pride. He loved the suddenly serious look in her eyes when she headed to work. And the deft movements of her hands as she treated patients, and the way she rolled up her sleeves a bit before she let her chakra flow. Sakura would always make notes for herself after conducting an examination, in addition to making up the patient's chart. Every time he witnessed the passion she had for learning, he felt that she also was doing everything she could for the village, but in a way that was different from how he did it, and that made him happy.

"I..." Staring at the lake before them, Sasuke said slowly, "I've never worried that someone might come along and take my place while I was away. Not once."

Sakura nodded and waited for him to continue.

"But sometimes, I get frustrated. Like when I come home for the first time in a while, and Sarada's gotten taller, or your hairstyle's changed."

"I feel the same sometimes," she replied quietly. "Like, when did Sasuke get those crow's feet around his eyes. Stuff like that."

"I have crow's feet?" He looked at her in surprise.

"When you smile, just faint ones. They're fine when you're scowling."

"You never change," he said and put a hand to her cheek. "You could have more wrinkles."

"What?" Sakura laughed, looking not displeased, and lowered her gaze. "Where's this coming from? Did someone say something to you?"

"No, I just wanted to tell you."

"Really?" She smiled. "I understand you only too well, Sasuke. We're fine."

I wish I could always be with Sakura like this, he thought from the bottom of his heart. But the fact was they couldn't be. Not with their different responsibilities and roles to play. The people of the village needed Sakura, and Sarada had dreams that she'd never be able to realize outside of the village of Konohagakure. And Sasuke didn't know any way to be useful to the village besides helping Naruto from the shadows by breaking new ground on missions.

"Okay." Sakura pulled Star Lines cards from her pocket. The six cards that made the Earth hand. "Let's hurry and get these ultra particles and go back to the village."

"Right." Sasuke nodded.

Sakura began to move her hands, referring to the images on the cards.

Sasuke's eyes stopped on the motif on the back of the picture cards. A lizard that resembled Meno coiled around a rock. Hadn't there also been a similar picture on the cover of *Map of the Heavens*?

"Why a picture of a lizard?" he asked abruptly.

"Huh?" Sakura looked up at him, eyebrows raised.

"There's no lizard in the *Map of the Heavens* constellations."

Looking at the back of the card, Sakura nodded, as if understanding. "It's probably not a lizard and a rock. It's a dragon and a meteor."

"A dragon...and a meteor?"

"A long time ago, a lot of dragons used to live around this area. They supposedly went extinct because of a meteor impact. That was tens of thousands of years ago, though, so probably no connection with the Sage of Six Paths."

Now that she mentioned it, there had been a note about how fossils could be dug out of certain geological layers in the ground here in that book that Penzila had been reading.

Fossils?

The basement room with its massive rock fragments flashed through Sasuke's mind. What if they were dragon fossils that the prisoners were made to dig up? And what if the Orochimaru who made off with this country's books was the same snake man that Sasuke knew?

Sakura brought her hands together in front of her chest. As she checked the pictures on the six cards, she slowly wove the signs one after the other.

The dinosaurs that went extinct because of a meteor.

The chickens and fossils collected in the basement.

And the jutsu developed by Orochimaru—Edotensei.

Lining these three elements up, Sasuke felt a shiver run down his spine.

What if Zansul's aim was to restore the dragons from the fossils? Using DNA extracted from the dragon remains, he sacrifices chickens, their direct descendants, to bring the dragons back to life. On paper, it was plenty possible.

The starry sky suddenly vanished from the lake. The surface of the water began to churn. He lifted his gaze with a gasp just as Sakura finished weaving the last sign beside him.

The water flashed, and a pillar of light shot up from the bottom of the lake, so dazzlingly bright he could hardly keep his eyes open. Slowly rising up in the center of that pillar was a bamboo vessel sealed with many overlapping protective wards.

"Are the ultra particles...inside of this?"

When Sakura reached for the vessel, half in disbelief, the pillar of light abruptly vanished, and the lake before them was placid once again.

She timidly touched the ward-laden surface and then yanked her hand back. "An unbelievable amount of chakra."

"What?"

He touched the vessel lightly, which was enough to make his skin tingle with a strange pressure. Only a true master could imbue wards with this amount of chakra. He and Sakura couldn't simply pop the vessel open to see what was inside, but he felt pretty confident that it contained the ultra particles sealed away by the Sage of Six Paths.

They had finally completed their mission to obtain the ultra particles. However, Sasuke's head was full of something else.

"Sakura," he said suddenly. "Physically, what's the difference between a dragon and a lizard?"

"Huh?" Sakura asked in reply, looking baffled, as she gripped the ultra particles container. This question had nothing to do with anything. "What about dragons?"

"I want to know about the physical characteristics of dragons and lizards."

"Uh, okay. I guess the biggest difference from reptiles is that the rear legs of dragons grow straight down from their bodies. Lizards, their legs stick out to the sides, and they sort of crawl along busily on all fours. But dragons were bipedal and maintained their balance by shifting their center of gravity back and forth."

Sasuke recalled the time he fought Meno. Long head thrust forward, tail waving as he ran. Meno was definitely bipedal, shifting the center of gravity back and forth. Meno wasn't a lizard, he was a dragon brought back to life with Edotensei. This answered several questions Sasuke had had about Meno. His genjutsu hadn't worked on the lizard because Meno was already being controlled by someone else, with Edotensei.

Zansul was collecting fossils and chickens in the basement. He wasn't going to stop at Meno. He intended to reanimate even more dragons.

"Sakura. I'm going back—"

To the observatory, he started to say, and in that moment, there was a roar that made him wonder if the moon had cracked in half.

He whirled his head around to look up the slope and saw a part of the observatory enveloped in a massive dust cloud.

"What was that?" Sakura cried. "An explosion?!"

"No. Not an explosion," he replied.

One massive creature after the other leaped out from inside the dust cloud and up into the sky. Wings of skin like a bat's, beaks sharp as spears. And enormous claws just like Meno's.

"Are those...dragons?!" Sakura gasped. "How... They're supposed to be extinct."

"Zansul brought them back with Edotensei."

Sasuke had realized the truth a beat too late.

Zansul was using Edotensei to bring ancient dragons back to life in the modern age.

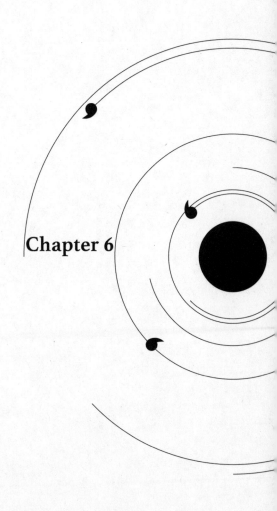

Chapter 6

Gaw! Gaw! The reanimated pteras flew above Sasuke's head, squawking loudly. There were at least ten of them.

He clicked his tongue at them and stopped his feet, which had been about to run back to the observatory.

"Sakura!" he shouted. "Go to the observatory and find Zansul!"

"What about you?!" she cried.

"I'm going after those dragons!"

Catching that group of fliers took priority. If they scattered and fled, even Sasuke wouldn't be able to go after all of them.

Sakura nodded and took off toward the observatory.

Sasuke was about to use Susano'o Flame Control to climb into the sky, but before he could, the enemy brought the fight to him.

A ptera landed before him, and Zansul slid off of its back, the same old easy smile on his face.

"So this is where you were, number four-eight-seven."

"Zansul..." Sasuke glared coldly at the director of the observatory. "It was you who brought the dragons back. To what end?"

"Heh," Zansul chuckled. "Why on earth would I tell you? I do have some questions I'd like to ask you, however."

"You won't answer mine, but you expect me to answer yours?" Sasuke said, hoping to draw out the conversation while he considered how he could make Zansul weave the signs to undo the jutsu.

The trouble was his fake eyes. Sasuke could stare as deeply as he wanted into a pair of glass eyes, but he could never cast an ocular jutsu on them. Could he use physical force, make the man weave the signs under pain of death? Whether Zansul would break under torture or not really depended on how loyal he was to the prime minister.

"It seems you don't understand your position," Zansul said. "You're nothing more than a shinobi separated from your country, but I have political power."

"Edotensei is a forbidden jutsu," Sasuke told him. "If you're going to act like you represent the country, then your country as a whole will be punished."

"Edotensei?" Zansul arched an eyebrow. "Is that what they call the forbidden jutsu to bring the dead back to life in your country?"

So the jutsu he was using wasn't exactly the same as the Edotensei that Sasuke knew.

Boom!

He heard a sudden loud rumble from behind, and then the sound of something clattering and crumbling. Most likely, part of the observatory wall had been smashed.

Had Sakura made it there safely? He glanced up at the top of the cliff, and Zansul's gaze followed in response. The man could clearly see Sasuke's movements. But not with his own physical eyes. He was getting his information on his surroundings through some other means.

Sasuke returned his gaze to Zansul. "Are you planning to use the reanimated dragons as weapons? To back the prime minister's conspiracy?"

"Oh, word travels fast. The fact that you know that means you also have comrades in Nagare then?"

"And if I did?"

"I'd be delighted," Zansul said. "It's an excellent opportunity to round up all of the prime minister's opponents in one fell swoop."

"Heh." The corners of Sasuke's mouth turned up. "Is slaughtering everyone here also part of the prime minister's plan?"

"What issue is there with that?" Zansul's face suddenly grew serious. "It's only natural that they should die. Despite having broken the laws of this country, they are granted life and live on carefree. The truth is I almost hate to send them to the bellies of my precious dragons, but I have no choice if I'm going to keep word about the dragons from getting out. I would never be out here supervising the nation's trash if not for the prime minister's plan. I have real political power—I'm the brains of this land. Not replaceable hands and feet like that lot!"

Growing more and more excited as he spoke, Zansul pushed up his glasses, which had slid down almost the length of his face to his lips, and cried ecstatically, "I would never have come to this place if not for the prime minister's plan!"

Zansul appeared deeply loyal. It was unlikely Sasuke could beat the information he wanted out of him.

Some other way...

He activated his Sharingan and turned eyes full of red light toward Zansul. He checked the amount of chakra in his body, and the tomoe floating in his eyes wavered in confusion.

The amount of chakra flowing through Zansul's body was absolutely no different than that of an average person. He was not a shinobi. There was no way he was the one using Edotensei.

What does this mean?

If it wasn't Zansul, then who brought back the dragons?

"What's the matter? You look a little pale." Zansul grinned, excitement still on his face.

In the next instant, Sasuke felt a murderous bloodlust in the air around him and leaped back.

Meno's fangs clamped down on the hem of his jacket.

A gliding ptera grabbed onto Zansul's collar and yanked him back up into the air.

"Meno, the rest is up to you," Zansul called as he flew away. "Finish him off!"

The reason Zansul jumped onto a ptera and sought me out was to keep me here for Meno to attack?

His Sharingan still activated, Sasuke faced Meno.

Orochimaru and Kabuto had controlled their targets with tags embedded in their heads, but he could see nothing of the sort on Meno's head. It seemed that this jutsu operated by a different mechanism from the Edotensei that Sasuke knew. And now that he was thinking about it, wasn't the jutsu that Orochimaru and his ilk used a refinement of the Second Hokage's proposed technique?

But reanimated beings using this refined jutsu were likely immortal in the same way as those reanimated with Edotensei. To stop Meno, Sasuke would have to restrain him without killing him, by using the black flames that only died when the target was incinerated: Amaterasu.

But if he did that, Meno would suffer endlessly, enveloped in an eternal conflagration, unable to die. If Sasuke was backed against a wall and left with no other choice, he would have to call on Amaterasu to get the job done, but he preferred to avoid that option if he could.

Long ago, his older brother had broken Kabuto's Edotensei with Koto'amatsukami, a genjutsu using the Mangekyo Sharingan of Uchiha Shisui. The ideal outcome would be for him to override the jutsu here in the same way. But he was up against an animal. Could it actually work against a creature without the intelligence of a human being?

"Meno," Sasuke called.

Meno crouched down in response. The black pupils that floated in his yellow irises narrowed sharply. Attack position.

"Don't move just yet. Stay calm and listen to my voice."

Sasuke took a slight step forward, and Meno opened his large maw and leaped at Sasuke like a spring coil being released. Sasuke drew his sword and stopped Meno's fangs with the scabbard. The lizard grew excited and clawed at the sword with his front leg to try and break it.

Sasuke could see a fresh scar where the oil had burned Meno's stomach. It seemed that he was slow to recover from burns, unlike cutting and stabbing wounds.

"Go ahead and chew on it." Sasuke slowly let go of the scabbard and reached a hand toward Meno's stomach.

The watchful lizard crunched through the scabbard.

"Relax. It's okay. I won't hurt you." Sasuke held his hand against Meno's belly and worked his chakra in his fingertips. He produced ice by super-chilling the mist made from Water Style with Wind Style.

Surprised by the sudden cold, Meno flinched.

"Shh." Sasuke covered Meno's burn. The ice crackled and settled, protecting and cooling the affected area.

Meno shivered and cocked his head, as if peering at Sasuke's face. The hostility had faded from his eyes. Or so it seemed.

"Meno, I apologize for cutting your stomach." Sasuke slowly reached out to the beast's damp nose. "It hurt, didn't it? I'm sorry. I won't do it again."

In the next instant, Meno yanked his mouth open. Sasuke could have dodged the bite, of course, but he dared to let him clamp onto his right arm.

Snorting, Meno closed his mouth, eager to bite and crush Sasuke's arm.

"Meno," he said, his arm still in Meno's mouth. "It's only natural that you're angry. Forced awake when you're happily asleep—

there isn't anyone alive who wouldn't be annoyed. I mean, I'd tear the person who did it limb from limb."

Meno grunted quietly, mouth still around Sasuke's arm.

"Hey? Don't you want to go back to where you were and sleep peacefully? I can send you back there. But to do that, I need your help."

Meno's breathing became quiet. The eyes that were narrowed sharply like pine needles grew somewhat rounder and turned up curiously at Sasuke.

The moment their eyes met, Sasuke focused his power in his eyes.

Sharingan!

Meno was already under the control of Edotensei. But with the power of Sasuke's eyes bearing down on him, his body twitched ever so slightly, and Sasuke felt hope that this might actually work.

Meno's jaws loosened, and Sasuke thrust the arm further into the beast's mouth, grabbed the long tongue, and poured chakra directly into the mucous membrane. Meno gagged and flailed, and then became suddenly quiet, like his strings had been cut.

Did I manage to overwrite the control with genjutsu?

He had only ever had a few chances to use genjutsu on non-human subjects, so he wasn't entirely certain it had worked.

He released the tongue in his hand, and Meno slumped over onto the ground. The long tail twitched.

"Meno," he said.

Meno slowly lifted his eyelids, and hazy yellow eyes focused on Sasuke's face. Instantly, his tail snapped out.

Bam!

Meno kicked at the ground and charged at Sasuke. He started to reach for a kunai to meet the attack, but then he noticed a slight change in Meno's eyes and let the tension drain out of his body.

Meno threw his front legs up into the air and brought the weight of his body down on Sasuke's shoulders. Sasuke didn't resist and allowed himself to be knocked over backward to the ground.

Meno threw himself on top of Sasuke and began to lick away the blood oozing from the bite marks on Sasuke's arm.

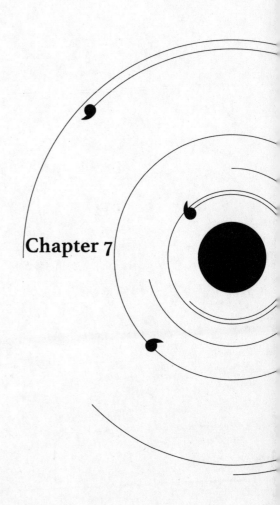

Chapter 7

"Eee! Let go, stop. Ah, aah. Ah, aaaaaaaah!!"

"What the hell are these things?! Where'd they come from?!"

"Stop. Stay away, don't, don't. Aah, stay back, stay—" The confused cries of prisoners.

Mysterious—and enormous—monsters crawled out from the massive rift in the courtyard and attacked anyone nearby.

Suddenly being slaughtered, the prisoners began to scream in terror.

"What are they?! Where are they coming from?!"

After being resurrected in the secret basement directly below the courtyard, the dragons had pushed through the ceiling to make their way outside. But the prisoners had no way of knowing all of this and had absolutely no idea what was happening. All they could do was run for their lives.

The spinos came out after the pteras. They were small dragons, about the height of a human being. They made optimal use of their maneuverable bodies as they jumped up and bit into heads and faces. One bite was enough to satisfy them, however, and they quickly moved onto their next target while the head-injured prisoners writhed in agony on the ground, mortally wounded but still alive.

The residential building was a hovel to begin with, and it collapsed easily under a barrage of headbutts from the pachycephalors. The prisoners who were slow to flee were crushed in the ruins of the building, but that was perhaps a more fortunate death. At the very least, they died without fear and extended suffering.

The pachycephalors had thick, hard, dome-shaped heads that they lowered as they charged their prey in straight lines. A fleeing prisoner tripped and fell, and the prisoners behind him all stumbled over his prone body and fell like dominos. The pachycephalors rushed the pile of fallen prisoners, some dozen people, trampling some, headbutting others. All of them died instantly.

The ones who survived this moment continued to flee until they reached the wall that surrounded the observatory and found that they had nowhere left to run.

"Dammit."

The wall on the south side was already half destroyed thanks to the hard head of a pachycephalor, but it was still almost entirely intact on the north side. One man tried to climb it using the person near him as a stepping stone but was clawed back down.

A pachycephalor took a menacing step forward and crouched down.

"Ah! Aaah! I'm done for!" A prisoner slumped down on the spot in despair, while another wept and beat at the wall.

The pachycephalor pushed its iron-hard head forward and charged. The men silently braced for their deaths.

"Oh yeeeah!!"

In tandem with this sudden cry, the wall behind them crumbled and fell away. And the doctor from the infirmary came racing through from the other side of the dust cloud.

The prisoners poured through the hole in the wall. Screaming and yelling, they scrambled to be the first to get outside.

The pachycephalor froze in confusion, and in the next instant, it took a powerful blow to the jaw and hit the ground.

Sakura turned to the main building as she shouted for the prisoners to escape to the outside of the wall.

The dragons would still come after them whether they fled or not, but they had a better chance at survival by running than they did clumping together up against the wall.

She could hear moans and cries of pain everywhere and saw many writhing in pain, on the verge of death. As a medical ninja, it was almost impossible to simply walk by them, but in that moment, her call to duty was to save the many over the few. She had to choose sacrificing these lives for the sake of saving the most prisoners as possible. She had to find Zansul right away and make him release the jutsu, or there would be even more casualties.

She had no extra time for the stairs, so she concentrated her chakra in the soles of her feet and ran up the wall, heading straight for the director's office. She kicked out a window and climbed inside, but there was no sign of anyone in the room. She checked his desk and bookshelves but couldn't find any documents related to the reanimation jutsu.

"Where on earth…" She frowned and then decided to search with a fine-toothed comb from the fourth floor all the way down to the basement.

As she slipped down the long corridor and descended to the third floor, she encountered a group of prisoners huddled on the landing. They had apparently arrived here in their flight from the rampaging dragons outside.

"It's too dangerous in here. You need to escape through the wall. Run as far away as you can." Sakura urged the prisoners outside and then checked the rooms on the third floor from one end to the other. The observation room, reading room, the guards' private chambers. Zansul was nowhere to be found.

She had to find him. The number of victims would only increase with every passing minute.

She hurried down the corridor and turned the corner, where she bumped into someone.

"Jiji!" she said.

"Doc? You're okay. Sure am glad for that." Jiji let out a sigh of relief. "But what is this? What's going on? I seriously don't know which way's up. Where'd those huge monsters come from?"

"It's the director's work," Sakura explained quickly. "He used the fossils to revive the dead and brought back the dragons. I have to find him and get him to release the jutsu."

"If you're looking for Zansul, he was in the courtyard a minute ago."

"What?" She stared at Jiji in surprise. "He's outside?"

Use of a high-level jutsu like Edotensei required a stable environment. She had assumed that the user would be hidden away from prying eyes somewhere in the observatory. But it seemed that she had misread the situation.

"Thanks, Jiji. You should hurry and get out of here too."

"Yeah, I'll be doing that." Jiji nodded but then yanked hard on Sakura's arm.

Caught off guard, she staggered and fell against his chest and felt an abrupt, sharp pain in her spine.

"What...?" Sakura dropped to her knees and slumped forward.

The kunai stabbed into her back clattered to the floor.

"Sorry, Doc."

Thump!

Her heart pounded heavily, and the core of her being shuddered. Her pulse throbbed in her ears, and her feet and hands were suddenly freezing cold. In contrast, her insides seized like they were on fire. She felt like all the cells in her body were boiling.

These symptoms.

They were the same as when Sasuke was poisoned by Meno.

"You were...working with Zansul..." Sakura could only move her eyes. She glared up at Jiji.

"I was. Even after we learned you were working with Sasuke, we strung you along. We couldn't solve the mystery of *Map of the Heavens* ourselves." Jiji crouched down and pulled the vessel with the ultra particles from her pocket.

"Give that...back..." She desperately forced a numb, trembling hand to clutch Jiji's ankle.

She couldn't let him have the ultra particles. She'd promised Naruto that she would return with Sasuke and a clue.

Jiji clucked his tongue and kicked her in the face. Sakura slammed into the wall, causing her head to split and crack. The shock of the impact raced up her spine all the way to the top of her head. She was less and less able to move by the second. Forget standing up; it was all she could do to keep breathing.

"Hah...! Haah...!" she panted.

"Personally, I really do think you're great." With dark eyes, Jiji peered at her face and went on apologetically. "You remind me of my girlfriend—your voice, the way you move. I do honestly feel bad you're going in this place. But you're not Margo."

He wove signs in front of his chest, and the earth shook beneath them.

The rupture in the courtyard ripped open even further, tearing up the almond tree by the roots before it could welcome its first blossoms with the coming spring.

An enormous snake-like creature covered in scales crawled up from a hole in the ground.

"What is *that*..."

Huddled together, the prisoners looked up at the monster, so massive that it nearly blocked the moon from view. The head and neck attached to the snake torso were at least ten meters long together, matched on the other end by a tail of the same length.

A titan, the most powerful dragon in all of history, gazed down on the four stories of the observatory.

Awakened from a sleep of tens of thousands of years, the enormous creature raised its head to the heavens as if stretching. Its long tail swung out and tore through the residential building, knocking the heavy roof tiles up into the air like droplets of water that then rained down on the area.

"That thing's so ridiculously huge that it destroys everything near it with even the smallest movement," Jiji remarked. "It wasn't revived until the very last."

The gigantic beast brought a foot down with an earth-shaking thud, and the entire observatory shifted suddenly. Unable to bear the weight of the mammoth creature, the building's foundations had crumbled.

The room bent and twisted, and cracks raced across the ceiling. Before her eyes, the fissure snaked all the way out to the hall. The plaster walls peeled and fell away like wafers.

Jiji set a foot on the window frame, and the massive beast lowered its head to welcome the ninja. He jumped down onto it and looked back at Sakura.

"Later, Doc."

The ceiling boards disintegrated, and the pieces rained down on the prone Sakura.

"...!"

With her body ignoring her desperate commands for it to move, she was swallowed up by the rupture in the floor and slammed into the stairs a story below. Roof tiles hit her in the face, a falling wall pinned her down, and her field of vision went black.

With Sakura still inside, the observatory collapsed with a roar.

•

His conspirator was Jiji.

Sasuke raced with Meno against the stream of fleeing prisoners and hurried to the observatory, slicing down all the dragons he encountered.

Zansul had referred to Kakashi as "your comrade." The only one who knew that Sasuke had a comrade was Jiji.

Zansul wasn't a shinobi. The one using Edotensei was Jiji. He had concealed his true nature so that Sasuke couldn't see that he was a shinobi. He had mastered a forbidden jutsu and had brought back to life multiple dragons at once. There was no doubt that he was a skilled ninja.

The observatory was in a terrible state. The wall, residential building, and library were all crushed. Only the main building was still standing, but just barely. The battered bodies of prisoners lay in piles everywhere, and dragons had their heads thrust into those heaps, feeding. In the chaos of everyone wildly trying to escape, Sasuke couldn't see any sign of Sakura. If she was looking for Zansul, she would have been in the main building.

"Meno, we part ways here. You help the prisoners escape. Get as many out as you can. Okay?" He turned toward the main building.

At the same time, there was a tremendous trembling of the earth.

The rupture in the courtyard turned into a ravine, and an enormous dragon, likely thirty meters long, appeared from below. The foundation was crushed under its weight, and the walls of the main building cracked and snapped. And then the whole courtyard collapsed.

Every other thought flew out of his mind.

His wife was still inside the observatory.

"Sakura!" Sasuke leaped into the cloud of dust and shoved aside rubble. "Sakura! Where are you?!"

He got no reply.

He looked with his Sharingan, but he couldn't detect any trace of her chakra and panicked even more. If he didn't know exactly where she was in this mess, he couldn't simply knock the rubble aside.

Sakura was no average jonin. Normally, being trapped under this amount of rubble would have given her little trouble. But not so if she couldn't use her chakra.

The poison painted on Meno's claws. If the same poison was used on Sakura she wouldn't be able to get out of this collapsed building using her own strength. Having experienced the poison himself, Sasuke knew that better than anyone else.

"Dammit..." He bit his lip in frustration.

Wasn't there any way to find her?

He racked his brain desperately, but in his frantic state, he couldn't think straight. In the end, all he could do was dig at the mess of bricks and wood before him.

"Answer me! Sakura!"

When Sakura came to, the first thing she saw was a peeling plaster wall. The tip of a nail poking out from it had stopped two centimeters from her right eye.

I...What happened...

Digging into her hazy memories, she remembered that she had gotten pulled into the collapse of the observatory.

When she turned her gaze downward, she found a large pillar lying across her lower body. She could sense wetness along the back of her thighs, but she couldn't determine where the bleeding was coming from. When she breathed in, an unpleasant sensation rose from deep in her chest, like her internal organs were twisting around.

Very tentatively, she tried moving. Her left hand was stuck, caught under something, but she could move her right hand. She pushed on the piece of wood in front of her, and it slid away so that her field of vision opened up just a bit. The narrow slice of night sky was clear on the other side of the dust, framed by the remains of the building.

She tried to knead her chakra, but there was absolutely no reaction from the chakra channels that should have been active inside of her. This was bad. Her body was numb, unmovable, and only wheezes came from her throat when she tried to call out. She couldn't make any sound. And if she couldn't work chakra, Sasuke's Sharingan wouldn't be able to find her.

She would have to get out of here on her own.

"Ngh!"

Sakura forced her twitching arm to move and tried to push away the pillar weighing down on her body.

The instant it moved the tiniest bit, she heard a clattering as something slid down somewhere else, and her hand froze. If she moved this chunk of what had been the observatory, another part of the wreckage might come crumbling down. Given that she didn't know if anyone else was buried there with her, she didn't dare push the pillar any further.

She was trapped.

"Hah... Hah..."

She panted, her vision growing pale and hazy.

It was impossibly frustrating that she was stuck here like this, helpless, while reanimated dragons were attacking prisoners outside.

Her pulse faded to a muted tapping, and the world around her became almost terrifyingly quiet. Her limbs were cold as ice, almost like she was dying slowly from her extremities inward. The cells in her body were utterly exhausted and wanted nothing more than to stop functioning.

No... If I pass out now, I'll die...

Sakura bit her lip and tried desperately to remain conscious, but she couldn't do anything about the strength leaving her body.

As a medical ninja, she was well aware that this wasn't the sort of poison that could be overcome through sheer willpower.

Cherry-pink eyelashes slowly veiled her field of vision.

Her consciousness sank to the bottom of her brain.

"Sakura!"

The familiar voice yanked her fading consciousness out from the abyss.

She slowly opened her eyes and found the face of the person she wanted to see most in this world there before her.

The weight pressing down on her body had disappeared. All of the wreckage around her had been cleared away, and she was being held up, supported by Sasuke's shoulder.

Sasuke, she tried to say, but her chest was on fire, and no words came out. Still, she had to tell him what she knew. She forced air through her vocal cords.

"Ji...ji...betray."

"Don't talk," Sasuke said curtly and touched the wound on her back.

The chakra he sent to the palm of his hand flowed into her with a mild heat, eliminating the poison and the havoc it was wreaking on her body, and warmth returned to her frozen limbs. But the pain suddenly sharpened, and she felt it stab at every part of her body.

"Can you move?" he asked.

"Mm hmm..." Her throat still wouldn't do what she wanted it to. Nonetheless, she managed to produce a confirming groan, and Sasuke's face finally relaxed the tiniest bit.

"Sasuke..." she whispered. "You came. Thanks..."

Relieved, the tears she'd held back finally spilled out of her eyes.

"Sorry... I couldn't stop Jiji... Couldn't do anything."

"Don't apologize when you're in this sort of condition."

The look on Sasuke's face made Sakura feel incredibly guilty when she thought about how she had worried this man. But more than anything else, she was relieved that he was there with her. When she had thought that she might die, the thing that had scared her the most was not seeing Sasuke and Sarada again.

The wound on her back slowly closed over, and familiar fingertips wiped her damp cheeks.

•

"Magnificent." Standing on the back of the enormous beast, Zansul looked down on the fleeing prisoners and snorted with laughter. Jiji was there beside him. "What a glorious feeling. The plan we spent so much time on has at last come to fruition."

"That it has," Jiji agreed, looking down on the miserable spectacle with cold, hard eyes.

The orniths made liberal use of their unbelievably powerful rear legs, each of which was about double the height of a person, and kicked up dust as they chased the prisoners down. Covered in brown feathers, the creatures looked exactly like ostriches.

They mowed everything down with their back legs. Prisoners struck directly were ripped open like water balloons filled with blood and transformed into mere clumps of flesh in the blink of an eye. Zansul watched as sharp talons caught one man in his side and then sliced open his back, leaving him to writhe in agony on the ground covered in blood.

"How unsightly." Zansul frowned. "Jiji, give him peace."

Without a word, Jiji looked down at the massive beast they rode on, and the snake-like dragon raised a leg as thick as the trunk of an ancient tree. *Thud, thud.* It stepped forward and casually crushed the suffering man. Orniths kicked the bodies of prisoners dozens of meters into the air, killing other prisoners when they were crushed under the falling corpses.

Zansul stared enraptured at the blood spurting up on the dry earth.

"What wonderful warriors. I'm certain the prime minister will also be pleased," he said and tilted his head back to look at the colossal creatures far above them. "Once we slaughter all the prisoners, we'll head for the capital and join up with him."

"That's all well and good, but don't forget your promise to me," Jiji reminded him.

"Of course not. Once we kill Nanara and the others, we'll go to Nagare and look for the body of your girlfriend. I do not forget a favor. It's thanks to you being able to use chakra and implement this reanimation jutsu that we have obtained all this battle power."

On the ground, an ornith was dragging its long neck along the earth, sniffing intently. It picked up a scent and trotted toward a pile of stone from the collapsed wall. It bent the talons of its front legs and deftly shoved aside the rubble to reveal Ganno crouched down there, shaking.

"Oh my. I believe he was your cellmate, yes?" Zansul turned happy eyes on Jiji, and he nodded wordlessly as he crossed his arms and looked down on Ganno.

"St-stay back!" Ganno's legs gave out under him, and he scooted himself backwards. His right foot was bare—maybe he had lost his shoe in the chaos. The bright red that adorned the nails on the toes of his hairy, wrinkled feet seemed to belong to another time and place.

The ornith slowly lifted its leg and brought it down toward Ganno's skinny body.

"Aaaaaaaa—"

His shriek was abruptly cut off.

Fresh blood dripped.

After a moment's silence, the ornith's foot left its leg and tumbled to the ground.

"What?" Zansul frowned.

Meno stood between Ganno and the ornith. He sprang at the chest of the bird-dragon as it lost its balance with the loss of its foot and bit into it.

"Graw!"

Letting out a shriek and toppling over, the ornith writhed and tried to throw Meno off. The lizard sank his fangs into the long, flailing neck.

Hearing the cries of its fellow, another ornith flew at Meno's back. But just as the ornith was about to strike him, Meno dodged, and the creature slammed into its wounded comrade. The two orniths tumbled over and rolled fifty yards, crashing through a number of people unfortunate enough to be in the way. They finally stopped when they smashed into the wrecked remains of the residential building.

"Jiji, what's going on?" Zansul cried. "Why is Meno taking the side of the prisoners?!"

Jiji checked the state of the reanimation jutsu he had cast himself and finally noticed the abnormality. "The control over Meno's been released."

"Sasuke?"

"Probably."

While the ornith was occupied by Meno, Ganno ran.

Zansul suppressed the urge to click his tongue in annoyance and quickly recovered his good mood. "Well, fine. They can't hurt us merely by taking Meno."

"I hope not," Jiji said.

Meno waged fierce battle with the ornith, ignoring the fact that it was several times larger. Slipping past its kicks, Meno leaped at the ornith boldly and bought time for the prisoners to flee. However, when at first it was one against one, it soon became two against one, and then three against one, until finally Meno was surrounded by five orniths.

Meno had nowhere left to run. An ornith closed in, swinging its leg out to kick.

Chak!

Sasuke's scabbard stopped the descending leg. He pushed back with the sheath, and the ornith somersaulted backward with one foot still up in the air.

"Good work buying time." Meno grunted happily at Sasuke's praise.

Sasuke took up position to guard Meno's back from the orniths and asked quietly, "What do you think, Meno? If it's too much for you, I can take care of these birds."

Meno pawed at the ground as if to say, "Don't be ridiculous."

Sasuke smiled slightly and said, "I'm right behind you."

The two of them kicked at the ground together, and in the next instant, the ornith's talons raked through the air.

"It's not effective to face them squarely. Get some distance and let the enemy come to you."

The orniths had one-track minds, and they charged at Meno. When Meno pulled back, their movements were simple and easy to read.

Meno watched for the right moment, as instructed by Sasuke, and sank down low. The talons that came at Meno sliced through empty air above his head. The force of the empty strike knocked the ornith off balance.

"Now!"

Meno stepped in close to the enemy and ripped out its throat. Everything from the neck up was freed from the torso, and the ornith threw out its legs and dropped to the ground. But dust quickly collected around the wound, and it began to heal. Sasuke stabbed the creature with his long sword to pin the head and body to the ground.

Before Meno had a chance to breathe, a mass of reddish brown came flying at him from the side.

A tyranno, the most powerful and malevolent of the dragons whose fossils were found in this region.

Held down by its incredible strength, Meno flailed and writhed. But the size difference between them was too great, and Meno couldn't break free.

Seeing the tyranno holding Meno down below him, Zansul narrowed his eyes, pleased. "A battle between members of the same species, but it doesn't look like it will get too heated, hm?"

"Same species?" Jiji asked, surprised. "Meno and the tyranno?"

"Yes, Meno is also a tyranno. Still a juvenile though."

When Jiji looked at the two with this new knowledge, he could see that their skeletons were actually very similar. The tyranno looked reddish brown because it had been showered in blood splatter, but its actual skin appeared to be the same grey as Meno's.

Jiji didn't know anything about ancient creatures. He had been chosen as Zansul's accomplice because of his abilities as a shinobi. Put another way, Zansul was utterly unfamiliar with the ways of the shinobi.

"It's a cruel thing to pit Meno against a fully grown animal. Or perhaps Sasuke isn't strong enough to assist him."

"Nah," Jiji said. "It's probably the tyranno that's at a disadvantage."

Zansul frowned, baffled. "What do you mean?"

Up against the muscular tyranno, Meno looked very tiny. Given that they were creatures of the same species, with a big difference in size, it seemed like the contest had been decided before the battle even started.

However...

With a roar, Meno pushed the tyranno back.

"What?!"

The tyranno was overcome and flipped over.

Before Zansul's surprised eyes, Meno bit into the stomach of the tyranno as hard as he could. The larger dragon writhed, rolling this way and that to try and shake Meno off, but Meno only dug his sharp fangs in deeper.

"Absurd," Zansul gasped. "Meno pushed it over?"

"When they're summoned, Kuchiyose creatures receive a supply of chakra from the summoner," Jiji explained coolly. "Meno made a contract with Sasuke and is receiving chakra from him. It's only natural that he'd be stronger than the other dragons."

Kuchiyose summoning built a mutually beneficial relationship between summoner and summoned; it wasn't a unilateral jutsu where one side got all the help. The summoner lent the summoned power, and by gaining the power of chakra, the summoned became even stronger.

"Sasuke's power is an unknown variable," Jiji said. "I don't think we can win unless we throw all of them at him."

"You should have said that sooner." Zansul glared at Jiji and then heard a shout from the direction of the observatory.

"Oh yeeeah!!"

Followed by *boom!* The sound of rock shattering.

The barely standing western wall crumbled thunderously, and that was the end of the wall that had once surrounded the observatory.

"It seems there's another rat," Zansul snarled. "Leave this to me. You go handle that."

"Right. This time, I'll finish her off for sure." Jiji turned his gaze up toward the sky, and a ptera flew down and scooped him up. They flew after Sakura as she fled past the ruined wall.

"So this is what you call biting the hand that feeds you," Zansul muttered, disgusted, and glared at Meno.

Blood dripping from his fangs, the small dragon stared with cold yellow eyes at the man he used to submit to. Behind him was prisoner number 487—Sasuke.

"I'll make you regret switching masters." Zansul raised his right hand.

At his signal, all of the dragons pivoted. The titan reared with a roar. The pteras circled, pulled their wings in, and dove. Even the orniths that had been pecking at the prisoners' corpses turned toward Meno.

Every single dragon began to stampede toward Meno and Sasuke.

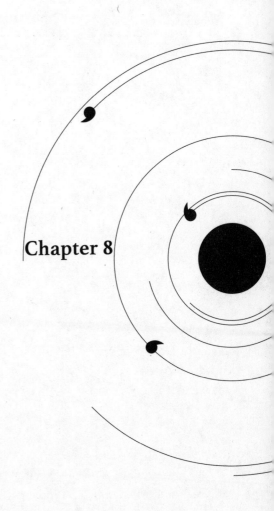

Chapter 8

Sasuke was about to muster a counterattack against the entire group of dragons, to clear them all away in one fell swoop with either Susano'o or Chidori. But when Meno stepped in front of him to try and protect him, he changed his mind.

"Meno," he said. "I'll draw off the little ones. You take down the big one."

In response, Meno raised his tail, full of self-satisfaction.

Sasuke wrapped his arms around the lizard, gave it a sign with his eyes, and then tossed it toward the titan. While he was at it, he hit the pteras soaring past Meno in the sky with a Lightning Style strike.

The pteras were knocked out and plummeted to the earth one after the other, and while one managed to evade the lightning strike, it ultimately collided head-on with an ornith, its eyes still blinded from the lightning. Its sharp beak stabbed deep into the ornith, and the angry bird-dragon kicked out blindly with both legs, striking with little regard to who was friend and who was foe.

Meanwhile, Meno had sunk his teeth into the tip of the titan's tail. Using his tail like a tightrope walker's pole, he closed in on Zansul.

"Don't let Meno near me!" Zansul cried out, but the top of its back was a blind spot for the titan. Neither its head nor its tail could even reach the spot where Zansul stood. "Ptera! Come and save me!"

One of the pteras wheeling in the sky heard this order and hurried to Zansul. It grabbed onto his collar with its beak just as Meno was about to attack and whisked Zansul up into the sky, leaving Meno's claws to slash at the air and rip into the titan's back.

The titan howled and twisted around to try and throw Meno off.

Meno didn't bother to resist. He dropped to the ground and ran in the direction that Sasuke had signaled with his eyes earlier. The titan chased after him with a stride ten times as long as Meno's.

Panting, Zansul pushed up his glasses. "To think that mere Meno could give me such trouble."

He was of course alarmed and angry that the creature Meno he thought was under his control had turned on him, no doubt at the suggestion of his new master. Number 487—Sasuke was chipping away at his precious battle power.

Zansul clucked his tongue and shouted thunderously at a nearby ptera. "You! What are you flying around for?! I told you to kill Sasuke."

That said, the area around the ninja was a free for all. Sasuke himself hadn't taken so much as a scratch, however. He nimbly dodged attacks as he lured dragons to strike each other.

Even though the dragons knew their frenzy only played to Sasuke's advantage, they couldn't disobey Zansul's orders, and so the pteras swooped down toward Sasuke. But before they could get close to him, they were hit with lightning strikes and dropped to the ground.

"Shouldn't push these dragons around too much, you know," Sasuke challenged Zansul as he caught the falling pteras with

Wind Style. "You're not the one using the reanimation jutsu—Jiji is."

"Nonsense!" A blue vein popped up on Zansul's forehead.

On Sasuke's instructions, Meno lured the titan away. Adroitly crossing from one rocky spot to the next, he descended on a diagonal. The titan was not the maneuverable type. Crushing the rocks that were its footholds, it lumbered after the smaller lizard.

Using a tyranno head as a launch pad to leap into the air, Sasuke checked that Meno had reached the edge of the lake and then cried out, "Cut its tendons!"

In response to this call from Sasuke, Meno changed direction. He slid under the belly of the titan and raced to the base of its tail to sink his fangs into its log-like leg. Without giving the monster the chance to even cry out in agony, Meno ripped out the flesh of the ankle together with the bone.

Helplessly, the titan bent heavily at the knee. Losing its balance, it fell over and plunged into the lake headfirst.

An incredible spray of water splashed up to the clouds.

"Useless waste of flesh," Zansul cursed. "Get out of that lake already!"

Blessed with buoyancy, the titan was quickly able to right itself. But the bottom of the lake was like a bog, and unable to support the weight of the titan, it quickly swallowed up its legs. Without a foothold, the titan couldn't crawl out, and so it was stuck there, unable to move, its head poking out above the surface of the water.

"Dammit! The huge body backfired," Zansul spat venomously and issued an order to the ptera carrying him. "Go down to the ground and pull that thing out of the lake!"

He didn't realize that he had given a fatal order.

The dragons could not take multiple orders from anyone who was not their summoner. And Zansul's command just now had overwritten his other orders—the dragon was now to go to the ground and rescue the titan. As a result, the ptera opened its beak and dropped its heavy burden to the ground to make itself lighter before gliding off toward the titan.

"Aaaaaah!"

Zansul slammed into the rocks in a burst of bright red like rose balsam. He bounced a few times, kept rolling, until he finally stopped, frozen and twisted.

Sasuke clucked his tongue and climbed down to check on the sand-covered Zansul, but there was no longer anything left of his original shape.

His abrupt end was due to his ignorance of reanimation jutsu.

The ptera in the sky above squawked once and circled around to the observatory. With Zansul's death, his orders were cancelled. The dragons scattered and began to target the prisoners once again.

"Meno, we have to hurry to the observatory."

Then, as if it had been watching for the moment when the dragons left, a hawk descended from the sky above. It was the bird they used to communicate with Kakashi. A letter was wrapped around its leg.

"A message at a time like this..."

Sasuke hurried to open it. A familiar hand wrote that the Kakashi-backed coup d'état had been a success, the prime minister had been captured, and he would be heading back to the capital with Queen Marina. Kakashi was apparently feeling a bit loose after this neat resolution; he even included a casual note about Nanara and the maid travelling with him.

So things were resolved in Nagare.

Sasuke stuffed the letter into his pocket and hurried toward the observatory.

•

Sakura beat back the dragons attacking her and bought time for the prisoners to escape.

She caught the rear leg of a charging ornith and did a shoulder throw to slam it into the ground. Two prisoners came racing up and jumped onto the fallen bird-dragon.

Ganno and Penzila.

They brought the hoes in their hands down on the backs of the ornith's knees.

"Graw!"

The ornith threw its head back and tried to get away, but it couldn't stand up now that the bones in its knees had been smashed. But dust soon collected on its crushed joints, healing the injuries. With miserable looks on their faces, Ganno and Penzila brought down their hoes again and again, compelled to keep up with the pace of regeneration.

"Dammit! Quit healing!" Penzila cried. "You can't go fixing yourself!"

You're going too far, Sakura started to say and then closed her mouth. Both humans and dragons were similarly desperate.

The reanimated dragons looked like powerful monsters in the eyes of the prisoners. But the dragons were also frantic. The orniths and the pachycephalors were herbivores and did not have natural predatory instincts. However, they also couldn't disobey their reanimator's order to slaughter all the prisoners.

"Hah!" Sakura cried and caught a ptera plunging down from on high.

The pteras were also unsuited to battle. Their bodies were extremely light, having evolved for flight. They were long, nearly ten yards in length, but they didn't even weigh twenty-five pounds. Their lone weapon was their sharply pointed beak, but after cracking open the skulls of so many prisoners, their sole weapon was losing potency.

Even so, they were not permitted to retreat. Or die. The spirits brought back to life with Edotensei were under absolute control of their reanimator. A ptera would tangle with Sakura for a bit, they would push and pull at each other, and then finally the ptera would withdraw. It would spread its wings and start to escape into the sky, but the swarming prisoners would catch it and yank it back down to the ground.

The pteras were wild and desperate, and thrashed at the prisoners' heads. But even when the pteras were covered in blood, not one of those hands let go. The ptera rachis, having evolved from the finger-like bones of their front legs, were light like twigs and would break easily if the creature's wings were pinned behind its back.

At first, they would squawk and cry for help, but when the bones of their neck were beaten down and their airways blocked, they could only wheeze.

As soon as they were hurt, however, the dust of the reanimation jutsu would cover the wound and heal the creature. Meanwhile, the prisoners would frantically beat at them with rocks to keep them from recovering. It was endless torture on either side. Until the reanimation jutsu was released.

We must hurry and find Jiji and free these dragons.

The moment Sakura thought this, she was overcome with dizziness.

Dropping to her knees, Sakura felt an aura of bloodlust behind her and rolled to one side. The kunai that grazed her cherry-pink hair plunged deep into the ground.

"Jiji!"

Not even a heartbeat later, Sakura flipped around and leaped to her feet. She lifted a piece of rubble as big as she was tall and threw it toward Jiji.

He drew his sword and sliced it in two with his long blade. By the time the pieces clattered to the ground, Sakura was gone.

She ran...

Jiji sniffed contemptuously. At this late stage of the game, fleeing was pointless.

A ptera in the sky found Sakura descending the cliff and reported back to Jiji.

Her movements were sluggish. He wasn't sure just how she'd escaped from the wreck of the observatory, but it seemed that she hadn't recovered completely from the poison. Jiji wove signs as he ran and thrust a hand down to the ground.

"Earth Style! Mud Wall!"

A wall of earth rose up and blocked the way forward, forcing Sakura to stop. Jiji chased after her.

Backed up against the dirt wall, Sakura glared at him with sharp eyes. "What are you after?"

"Eeaugh!"

Jiji heard a shriek in the distance. He didn't know whether it was the cry of a person or a dragon.

"Making dragons and people suffer like this! What exactly is it that you want?!"

"I do feel awkward about striking you with a killing blow twice, Doc." And he really meant that. It was selfish, but he would have liked the doctor and Sasuke to survive, if possible. Now that it had come to this, however, he had to kill them.

I told Sasuke. Don't go leaving your wife alone.

Sakura took a step back and bumped into the wall of earth.

Jiji took a step forward.

Bang!

He suddenly couldn't move.

"?!"

By the time he realized he was in trouble, it was too late. His joints were firmly fixed in place, and he couldn't even wiggle his body.

A barrier. A trap lying in wait.

The sand at his feet blew up in the wind, revealing a ward with a curse mark carved into it. A thread of bright red chakra twined up to bind Jiji's body firmly in place.

The ward had clearly been set to activate a jutsu when the target passed over it. While pretending to run away, Sakura had been luring him here right from the start.

"Dammit."

Jiji pulled a kunai from his sleeve and cut at the chakra threads. But the threads only released the crackling chakra contained within. There was no place where he could cut himself free.

At some point, a mark patterned after a sakura petal had popped up on his wrist.

"When did you... This mark..."

"When you came to the infirmary. Just in case," Sakura said calmly. "I'm a doctor. I can easily tell just how much of a chakra user someone is when examining them."

Jiji struggled furiously to find a way out, but he soon realized that he would not be able to break away and relaxed.

Not yet. He hadn't lost yet. If Zansul joined up with him here, he could still get out of this. Or maybe there was a way to make Sakura release the jutsu. Negotiate, say that he would release the reanimation jutsu...

As he grasped for whatever chance at victory he had left, Jiji suddenly sensed an enormous amount of chakra around him, and a chill ran up his spine. His knees gave out. The pressure of this chakra was so intense that any remaining thought of escape was shattered in an instant.

"Jiji. You're the one behind the reanimation jutsu?" came a low voice from behind.

Appearing with Meno in tow was his cellmate, who up to that point had never once shown bloodlust like this.

Sasuke reached into the pocket of Jiji's coat and took back the vessel containing the ultra particles. He kept digging and found a yellow liquid sealed in plastic.

"Is this the drug you used on Sakura and me?" Pushing down the anger simmering up inside of him, Sasuke activated the Sharingan and faced Jiji.

"Those eyes," Jiji gasped when he saw the Sharingan. "You're Uchiha? You're not going to get Zansul with that. You've basically got the same chance at winning as I do."

Jiji met the red eyes of his own will.

"You're going to use genjutsu on me, yeah? Fine, do what you want. If you're going to do it, I want you to make it so I never wake up."

"I'm not letting you off so easily. You'll pay for what you've done, but there's something I want to ask you before I use my genjutsu." Sasuke drew his Sharingan back and lowered his voice as he continued. "What is your objective? Zansul's was to use the revived dragons as weapons of war. But you're not that type."

"That type?"

"The type to act on behalf of his country."

"Ouch." Jiji smiled lifelessly. "That's just your opinion. Maybe I was working with Zansul because I agreed with his convictions."

"In that case, why did you save Penzila?"

Jiji blinked slowly at Sasuke, uncomprehending.

"When Penzila was about to be attacked by Meno," Sasuke explained. "If you were going to get rid of all the prisoners, then why didn't you let him die then? Because you cared about Penzila? Or because you were reluctant to make Meno a tool of murder?"

"Neither, okay?" Jiji snapped. "I brought Meno back to life for that purpose. And I mean, Penzila—I'm not going to start caring about some guy just because he happens to be in the same cell as me. Not too long ago, I stood and watched when Ganno was about to be killed."

"But." Sasuke stared back at Jiji. "You acted instantly."

Sometimes, people were spurred on by feelings they weren't aware of and took action they didn't expect.

Even now, Sasuke clearly remembered when he had protected his close friend before he even realized he was doing it and leaped out in front of Haku's Thousand Stinging Needles of Death. At the time, he'd been deeply perplexed by his action, but now he understood it. They'd had any number of breaks between them, but from that time on, Naruto had been Sasuke's good friend, in a way that went beyond reason or logic.

He didn't think that what Jiji felt toward Meno, Ganno, and Penzila was the same as the feelings Sasuke had for Naruto. But at the very least, he must have had some kind of affection for them.

"Zansul is dead," Sasuke declared. "We're handing you over to the Land of Redaku and returning to our own country. But before that... If you have some exceptional circumstances, tell me now."

"Why should I?"

"I don't want to end this without knowing."

Beside Sasuke, Meno stretched out his neck, cocked his head slightly to one side, and stared at Jiji.

Jiji looked back and forth between Meno and Sasuke, and his expression relaxed with a sigh.

"Well, the plan's ruined now anyway," he muttered and began his story slowly. "I'm a rogue ninja from Sunagakure. I originally came to the capital after an invitation from the Land of Redaku's prime minister. This was back when the old king was still alive. The prime minister was hatching this plan to hire rogue shinobi and create a private army. He called me in to coach him on shinobi and ninjutsu. While I was staying at the palace, the prime minister assigned a personal maid to me. And I fell for her. Rather than be a part of some war, I wanted to live forever with her in the Land of Redaku."

"And the prime minister found out?" Sakura asked, and Jiji nodded.

"I guess someone saw us together. We got caught pretty quick. But the prime minister said that if I wanted to be with her, I didn't have to be in his private army."

"In exchange for your helping Zansul?"

"Uh-huh. Zansul was an archaeologist at the palace. He found a text about a jutsu to reanimate the dead in the library and succeeded at deciphering it. But even if he knew the method of the jutsu, Zansul couldn't use chakra. So I was called in to perform the reanimation jutsu. The agreement was if I worked with Zansul here at the observatory for a year, I could live however I wanted after that. I lied to my girlfriend and said that I'd been called up for a long-distance mission. I promised we'd meet again in the capital in a year. But before the year was up, she died."

Jiji stared at the ground with an exhausted look on his face.

"I was wrong. If I'd really loved her, I couldn't have left her. I shouldn't have left her all alone. ...Hey, Sasuke? I told you, didn't I? Don't go leaving your wife alone? That's how I really feel. People die so easily."

Meno grunted quietly. Whether he understood or not, the lizard was listening to Jiji, and Jiji glanced at him before lowering his eyes once more.

"I was told that the reason we were bringing Meno back to life was to have him act as a guard for the prisoners. I wasn't told the true objective until the day I found out my girlfriend was dead. Using dragons as weapons, I mean... At first, of course, I didn't want to. But Zansul and the prime minister made me an offer."

"An offer?"

"They'd get my girlfriend's body for me if I helped revive the dragons. And if I had her body, I could see her again."

"You were going to...bring her back to life with the reanimation jutsu." Sakura finished his thought.

Noticing the look on Sakura's face, Jiji grinned.

"Don't be hurt, Doc. And don't make that face at me. I just had to see her one more time. Even if I had to force a meeting with a forbidden jutsu... Sasuke, what would you have done in my position? You'd do the same thing, wouldn't you?"

"..."

Sasuke stayed silent, very much unable to say that he wouldn't have done that. He was remembering the time he'd been reunited with his older brother Itachi after Itachi had been brought back to life with Edotensei. Being able to talk with him for even a few minutes after clearing up their misunderstanding was one of Sasuke's most treasured memories, even if it required the use of a forbidden jutsu.

If his own wife passed away for some reason, he just might want to do the same thing as Jiji.

"Maybe."

It was Sakura who answered him.

"I mean, if Sasuke died and I had the Edotensei jutsu in front of me, I might reach for it. Out of desperation to see him."

"So then..."

You get how I feel, Jiji started to say, and Sasuke cut him off.

"But the two of us aren't alone. I know my friends would stop me. They'd tell me not to do anything stupid. We're stopping you for the same reason. And I'm sure that your girlfriend, Margo—she definitely wouldn't want to be forced back to life with a reanimation jutsu."

"Margo?" Sasuke lifted his face.

Margo. That was Jiji's girlfriend's name?

The letter he'd just gotten from Kakashi was still stuffed in his pocket. He pulled the creased paper out and sent his eyes over the text.

"Jiji, you've been here for over a year, right?" he said. "How did you find out Margo was dead?"

"A notice of her death came, addressed to me," Jiji replied. "In the prime minister's own hand. Some epidemic."

"The prime minister was in on it." Sasuke showed Jiji the letter from Kakashi. "It's here in this letter from my comrade. After toppling the dictatorship, the new king Nanara decided to transfer the queen and the prime minister to the capital. An attendant of the king, a woman named Margo, was originally a maid in the palace, so she's very knowledgeable about the situation inside. She's apparently been very helpful."

Jiji gaped at him. "What?"

"This is information from someone I trust," Sasuke told him.

Jiji's eyes devoured the text of the letter, then their focus wavered and wandered.

He couldn't properly digest this sudden development. Even so, after going over the letter a few times, tears began to spill from his eyes. They had lied and said Margo was dead to make Jiji do exactly what they wanted. Why hadn't Jiji realized that this was exactly the sort of thing Zansul would think up?

Tears slid down to his chin and dripped off to wet his thigh, but the sound of this was drowned out by that of a branch breaking.

Snap.

Jiji yanked his face up.

The tyranno had killed its aura enough to approach Sakura from behind unnoticed. But when it realized that Jiji had spotted it, the beast crouched low and sprang forward.

"Doc!"

Jiji immediately wove signs in front of his chest. Rat. Ox. Monkey. Tiger. Pig. Dragon. The signs to release the reanimation jutsu.

By the time he finished weaving the signs, Sakura had already reacted to the danger herself and was punching the tyranno in the jaw.

Crack!

The tyranno sailed up into the air and fell to the ground. It got up quickly enough, but the hard skin at the tip of its snout suddenly began to peel away. The bits of skin turned to dust and began to rise into the sky, not carried by any wind.

Now that Jiji had woven the signs for release, the dragons were freed from the reanimation jutsu.

The pteras that had been holding down the prisoners; the spinos crawling along the ground, their legs broken; the titan struggling in the cold water—the dragons that had been treading water for such a long time were at last liberated from their endless sleep and greed-filled control. Bit by bit, peacefully, their souls returned to the other side.

And of course, that meant Meno too.

The lizard grunted feebly, reluctant to leave. He pressed the gentle curve of his head against Sasuke's side and rubbed it up against him. The tail swinging from side to side fell away, the pieces dancing up into the air.

"You finally get to go back, hm, Meno?"

Sasuke stroked him under his chin, and Meno sighed and narrowed his eyes happily. He wrapped claws with visible veins tightly around Sasuke's waist.

"Good night."

His limbs and torso turned to dust bit by bit and rose to a place where there was no pain or struggle.

Sasuke felt flecks of cold against his cheek, and just when he was wondering if the dust of the reanimation jutsu was as icy as this, he realized it was snowing. The gently falling flakes mixed with the rising dust seen from below looked like the dance of gold and silver sand against a black curtain of gauze.

With the tomoe in his eyes, Sasuke could see everything, including how the thin crystals of ice reflected the light of the moon and sparkled like a rainbow.

After taking a crack in the jaw from Sakura, the tyranno stubbornly fought the providence of the release of the jutsu. Although its upper body was already more than half gone, the eyes of the tyranno were not giving up. It swung its long tail and forced itself to its feet.

Bam!

It kicked at the ground boldly with one foot and charged Jiji, perhaps to get revenge for having been put under his control, or perhaps because he saw Jiji as prey out of simple instinct.

But after letting his guard down with the release of the jutsu, Jiji's reaction was entirely too late.

Blood spurted as curved talons sank deeply into his chest, and the tips of those talons stabbed into his throat.

"Jiji!" Sakura cried.

Having gotten its vengeance in the end, the tyranno melted into the sky, showered in blood.

"Hang on!" Sakura ran over and released the chakra thread, while Sasuke caught him as he slumped backward.

Sakura was about to press her hand to his wound when Jiji's own bloody hand grabbed it.

"You...don't have to...treat me..."

"No!" She brushed his hand aside and sent out her chakra. "I mean, you're going to see Margo, right?! You just found out she's still alive!"

"Just leave...me...be..." His vision grew darker. "I...can't face her...like this... Go... The other guys..."

Choked by the blood in his throat and without the strength to even cough, Jiji couldn't push out another word.

The sound around him was warped like he was underwater. He let his eyelids slide shut, not fighting the steady, sinking weight of his body.

It was funny somehow to think that he would die here alone.

I thought I would die when they told me Margo was dead. Regretting the fact that I left her alone, that I wasn't always with her. I thought she died because I wasn't there to keep her safe.

But that was pure arrogance.

Off in the distance somewhere, Sakura and Sasuke were calling his name.

He was so jealous of them he could hardly stand it. If he had had the strength that they did, he was sure none of this would have happened. If he'd been able to believe in what wasn't there with him, what he couldn't see with his eyes.

It was too late for regrets now.

In the black depths of his world, Margo called out to him.

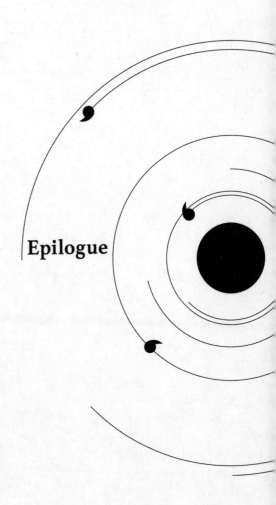

Epilogue

The new king Nanara set a bouquet of blue poppies on the memorial and pressed his hands together in prayer.

Engraved in the polished granite were the names of sixty-two prisoners, all those who had died in the terrible incident that happened in this place the previous year.

There was no sign of the former astronomical observatory. The buildings had been destroyed along with the ancient texts and expensive astronomical measuring instruments, and the rubble was still strewn about everywhere.

Lowering his hands, Nanara turned toward his two attendants. "Where's my sister?"

"She says she will finish her inspection in the north and arrive here tomorrow perhaps," replied the attendant with the chestnut-brown hair—Margo.

"I see." Nanara nodded. "I've been so focused on the capital and Nagare that I've completely put off rebuilding this place, even though astronomy is an important discipline for the Land of Redaku. We'll have to set it up again so that we'll be able to study not just the heavens but also excavate fossils. Do you think my sister would be angry if I said I wanted to establish an archaeo-logical institute alongside the observatory?"

"She might get angry. She'll say, 'Do you think money grows on trees? You have to think more seriously about how to use tax revenue!'" Margo sounded so like Marina that the attendant beside her laughed out loud.

She grinned and continued.

"But it's fine if she gets angry at you. So go ahead and suggest it."

"Right. You're exactly right, Margo!" Nodding vigorously, Nanara ran over to where his horse was resting under a tree. He set a foot into the stirrup, vaulted onto his horse's back, and turned to look back at his attendants.

One was the woman who had long taken care of him. And the other was someone he had brought along specifically to show them around this area, a model prisoner serving a life sentence.

"Let's go look at the lake next. Come on, Margo! Jiji!"

•

At a sunny table on the open patio of the popular Japanese-style café set up inside the traditional sweet shop Tami in the old city, Sakura met up with Ino.

They were both busy with work and home, but even so, a couple times a month, they would rearrange their schedules and meet for tea. They were close friends with plenty to talk about—the children, their work, their husbands.

"So the other day, I had some fun with Inojin's hair and the curling iron."

"What? Inojin must have hated that."

"He did, but I sort of forced him to let me. I mean, that boy takes after Sai—his hair's bone straight, isn't it? I went to all the trouble of styling it for him, and then it goes right back to the way it was."

"Huh. If he doesn't get bedhead, I might be a little jealous, actually. Oh! That reminds me. Temari told me that Shikamaru's bedhead is absolutely wild!"

"I know, I know. I saw it so many times when we were on missions. He looks like a porcupine."

They chatted excitedly about nothing in particular, while sampling the new menu item of *anmitsu* crepes topped with *sanshoku-dango* dumplings and *anko* sweet beans. Ino suddenly turned her face to one side. "Ah! It's Sasuke."

Was he on his way home after stopping at the Hokage's office? He was just walking along empty-handed, but his looks and the way he carried himself were so cool that he attracted attention no matter where he went.

Sakura watched him walk away and then threw herself down on the table, groaning, "Sasuke really is so hoooooooot."

"Huh? You just got the memo?" Ino turned exasperated eyes on her. "I mean, true. Sasuke is as hot as he ever was. But how many years have you been married exactly? You're only now feeling the hotness?"

"I mean..."

"And weren't the two of you on a long-term mission until just yesterday?"

"We were, but in the middle of a mission's no time to stare and drool," Sakura complained. "There's this switch in me that flips as a shinobi, so I'm not always just gawking stupidly at him. But when we got back to the village, it's like... It felt so fresh and new."

"Yeah, yeah. Fine. Mm hmm. Thanks for the crepe." Ino teased and cut into the chocolate-sauced crepe with a knife, and then grinned and leaned forward. "Hey! You never wear jewelry. What's with the ring?"

"Oh, this?" Sakura dropped her gaze to her left ring finger. Looking at the small red stone with fresh eyes, she giggled.

Ino narrowed her eyes in a smile. "That's great."

Strictly speaking, it was not really the definition of a present. But this ring was now Sakura's treasure.

Sasuke had made it by manipulating the ingredients in Earth Style, and mixed in with those was his own chakra. This ring was the reason he'd been able to find her when she was pinned down by that pillar and unable to move. He'd picked up on the faint amount of chakra the ring contained and worked his way down to where she was.

This ring had saved her life.

But it might get in the way at work.

After saying goodbye to Ino, Sakura smiled on her way home, took off the ring, and tucked it into her pocket.

Someday, when I'm an old woman, I'll retire from work. Then I'll have all the time in the world to wear the ring.

Until then, she'd treasure it and take good care of it. Sakura stroked the ring from the outside of her pocket.

Would Sasuke remember it when he was an old man?

Sarada made supper by herself that day.

She came home, arms laden with shopping bags, and abruptly declared, "I'm doing all the cooking today!"

She had apparently gotten very into cooking while on her homestay at Iruka's house.

"I made all kinds of things with Master Iruka, and I think my cooking's gotten a lot better!"

That evening, the Uchiha table was filled with far too many dishes for the three of them to be able to finish.

The main course was beef sukiyaki stir-fry with tomato, complimented with side dishes of stewed root vegetables, tomato and *okara* tofu salad, boiled broccoli, fried egg, and slices of mackerel pike fried with salt. On top of the rice neatly piled in their bowls was a mix of soy and bonito flakes combined with squash fried with minced chicken meat.

These were the impressive results of Sarada's full efforts, a sampling menu of all kinds of small dishes.

"Wow! What a spread!" Sakura cried. "And you made lots of Dad's favorites too!"

"Mm. Well." Sarada shrugged. "That's just a coincidence. The tomatoes were cheap today."

However coincidental it might have been, she had piled Sasuke's plate high with mostly tomatoes.

For the first time in a long time, the entire Uchiha family sat around their dining table together for a meal.

Sasuke simply ate without commenting on the flavor of anything, so Sakura gently kicked his ankle under the table.

"Hm?" Lifting his face, Sasuke met Sakura's eyes and froze for a moment before at last figuring out the meaning of the kick and stating his extremely simple opinion. "It's good."

"Huh?" Sarada said. "Really?"

"Yeah. It's good. Great."

As always, Sakura's husband's vocabulary was small. But his message came across.

"Honestly. You don't have to be nice just because I made it, you know," Sarada said, looking delighted nonetheless.

While they were eating, the doorbell rang.

"Oh! I'll answer it." Sakura pushed Sasuke back down as he started to stand up and headed for the front door.

When she opened it, Shikamaru was standing there with a thick folder in his arms.

"Sorry to bother you during suppertime," he said.

"Mm mm." Sakura shook her head. "It's urgent, I guess?"

"Yeah. Sarada sounds happy," Shikamaru remarked, glancing down the hallway.

"It's not just her. Sasuke too. It's been a while since the whole family was together."

"Sasuke too, huh?" Shikamaru frowned and held the folder out to Sakura. "Interim report on the analysis of the ultra particles from the institute. I wanted to get it to you."

"Thanks," Sakura said and took the folder from him.

Although they'd stopped Zansul, there was still plenty that didn't quite make sense to her. The sentence "the stars increased" in *Map of the Heavens*, the Konoha mark. The meaning of the star that never strays and how Zansul was able to see with his glass eyes. Any one of these might have had some connection with the Sage of Six Paths' illness, and she wanted to scrape together every bit of information she could, given that the target they were facing was an unknown variable.

"How's Naruto?" she asked, and Shikamaru shook his head.

"Not great. I keep telling him to rest, but he's there in the Hokage's office every day. And even when I deliberately give him less work, he finds new work on his own."

"Maybe it distracts him to be busy. And it doesn't seem like the kind of thing that's going to get better with just rest."

"True."

While they talked, Shikamaru kept glancing down the hallway. He was concerned that Sarada might come out.

They couldn't upset the children. They couldn't let word of this get out. Those were the conditions that Naruto had laid out when Shikamaru and the others had forced Naruto to agree to let them help him.

"I asked them to make the analysis a priority at the institute," Shikamaru said and sighed heavily.

The situation was such a drag that even saying what a drag it was was too much of a drag.

"If this keeps up, Naruto won't be able to use chakra anymore. We absolutely can't let that happen."

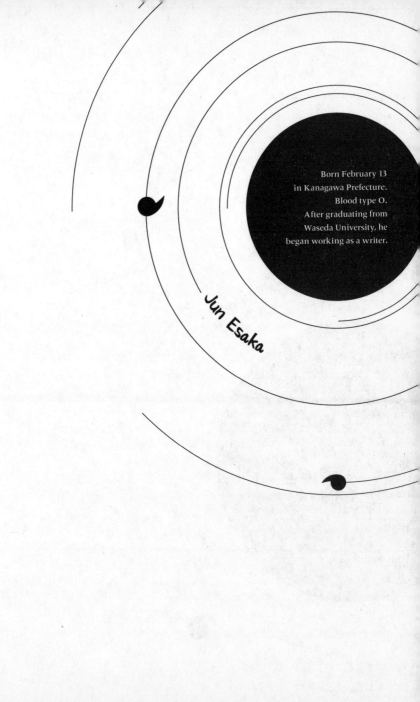

Born February 13
in Kanagawa Prefecture.
Blood type O.
After graduating from
Waseda University, he
began working as a writer.

Jun Esaka

Masashi Kishimoto

Author/artist Masashi
Kishimoto was born in 1974
in rural Okayama Prefecture,
Japan. After spending time in art
college, he won the Hop Step Award
for new manga artists with his manga
Karakuri (Mechanism). Kishimoto
decided to base his next story on
traditional Japanese culture. His first
version of *Naruto*, drawn in 1997, was
a one-shot story about fox spirits;
his final version, which debuted
in *Weekly Shonen Jump* in 1999,
quickly became the most popular
ninja manga in Japan.